HARDWATER

COUNTRY

HARDWATER COUNTRY

STORIES

FREDERICK BUSCH

Alfred A. Knopf   New York   1 9 7 9

This is a Borzoi Book
Published by Alfred A. Knopf, Inc.

I am grateful to the National Endowment of the Arts for its support.
Thanks go, as well, to the editors of the following magazines, where
some of the stories first appeared, sometimes in altered form: *Harper's*,
"The Old Man Is Snoring" and "My Father, Cont."; *Chicago Review*,
"Traveling Alone in Dangerous Places"; *Fiddlehead*, "Is Anyone Left
This Time of Year?"; *Bennington Review*, "Sunday, Late";
Ploughshares, "Company"; *Fiction*, "Small Talk, Prayers"; *Playgirl*,
"The Lesson of the Hôtel Lotti"; *The Paris Review*, "Widow Water";
The Mississippi Review, "Family Circle"; *Crazy Horse*, "The Land of
the Free"; *Story Quarterly*, "What You Might as Well Call Love";
The North American Review, "Long Calls."

Library of Congress Cataloging in Publication Data
Busch, Frederick [date]
Hardwater country.
I. Title.
PZ4.B9767Al 1979 [PS3552.U814] 813'.5'4 78-23745
ISBN 0-394-50560-3

Manufactured in the United States of America
First Edition

For my parents

HARDWATER

COUNTRY

W I D O W

W A T E R

What to know about pain is how little we do to deserve
it, how simple it is to give, how hard to lose. I'm a
plumber. I dig for what's wrong. I should know. And
what I think of now as I remember pain is the fat young
man and his child, their staggering house, the basement
filled with death and dark water, the small perfect boy on
the stone cellar steps who wept, the widow's coffee gone
cold.

They called on Friday to complain that the pump in
their basement wouldn't work. Theirs is shallow-well
country, a couple of miles from the college, a place near

the fast wide river that once ran the mill that all the houses of the town depended on. The railroad came, the town grew, the large white clapboard houses spread. By the time their seedlings were in the middle growth, the mill had failed, the houses had run to blisters of rotted wood on the siding and to gaps in the black and green roofs. The old ones were nearly all dead and the railroad came twice a day, from Utica to Binghamton, to Utica from Binghamton, carrying sometimes some freight, sometimes a car of men who maintained the nearly useless track. And the new people came, took their children for walks on the river to the stone foundations of the mill. They looked at the water and went home. People now don't know the water as they should. I'm a plumber, I should know.

I told him I couldn't come on a Friday afternoon in April, when the rains were opening seams and seals and cellars all through the county. Bella was making coffee for us while I took the call, and I snapped my fingers for her to turn around. She did, all broad—not fat, though—and full of colors—red in her face, yellow in her hair going gray, the gold in her tooth, her eyes blue as pottery—and I pointed at the phone. She mouthed a mimic "Today, today, today," and I nodded, and she nodded back and poured the almost boiling water out into the instant coffee, which dissolved.

He said, "So you see, sir, we can use your help."

I said, "Yessir, sounds like a problem."

"No water, and we've got a boy who isn't toilet-trained. It gets kind of messy."

"I imagine."

"So do you think you could . . ."

"Yessir?"

"Come kind of soon?"

"Oh, I'll come kind of soon. It just won't be today."

"You're sure you couldn't . . ."

"Yessir?"

"Come today?"

"Yessir."

"Yes sir, what?"

"Yessir, I'm sure I can't come."

Bella rapped on the table with her big knuckles to tell me to come and sit. I nodded, pointed at the telephone, waited for him to try once more. He was from the college—he would try once more.

He said, "But no water—for how long? The weekend? All week?"

I heard a woman whisper in the background with the harshness of a wife making peace, and then he said, "Uh —I mean, do you know when you can come?"

I said, "When're you up?"

"Excuse me?"

"When do you wake up?"

"We'll be up. Just tell me when."

I said, "I'll be there tomorrow morning, early, if that's all right."

"I mean, how early?"

"You get up, Mr. Samuels, and you have yourself a comfortable breakfast, and I'll be there for a cup of your coffee."

He hung on the line, waiting for more. I gave him nothing more, and he said, "Thanks. I mean, we'll see you tomorrow, then. Thank you."

"Thank *you* for calling, Mr. Samuels, and I'll see you soon."

He said, "Not soon enough," and chuckled and didn't mean the laugh.

I chuckled back and meant it, because coffee was waiting, and Bella, and a quiet hour before I went back out to clear a lonely lady's pipe in a fifty-foot well. I said, "Good-bye, Mr. Samuels."

He said, "Yes," which meant he was listening to his whispering wife, not me, and then he said, "Yes, good-bye, thank you very much, see you soon."

I blew on my coffee and Bella turned the radio off —she'd been listening to it low to hear if she'd won the fur coat someone in Oneida was giving away—and we sat and ate bran muffins with her blueberry jam and talked about nothing much; we said most of it by sitting and eating too much together after so many years of coffee and preserves.

After a while she said, "A professor with a problem."

"His pump won't turn off. Somebody sold him a good big Gould brand-new when he moved in last summer, and now it won't turn off and he's mad as hell."

"Well, I can understand that. They hear that motor banging away and think it's going to explode and burn their house down. They're city people, I suppose."

"Aren't they ever. I know the house. McGregory's old place near the Keeper farm. It needs work."

"Which they wouldn't know how to do."

"Or be able to afford," I said. "He's a young one and a new professor. He wouldn't earn much more than the boys on Buildings and Grounds. I'll bill him—he won't have the money in the house or at the bank, probably— and we'll wait a couple of months."

Bella said, "We can wait."

"We will."

"What did you tell him to do?"

"I told him to unplug the pump."

"He wasn't satisfied."

"I guess I wouldn't be."

"Abe," she said, "what's it like to be young as that?"

I said, "Unhappy."

She said, "But happy, too."

"A little of that."

She bent her gray and gold head over the brown mug of dark brown coffee and picked at the richness of a moist muffin. She said, still looking down, "It's hard."

I said, "It gets easier."

She looked up and nodded, grinned her golden tooth at me, said, "Doesn't it?"

Then I spent the afternoon driving to New Hartford to the ice-cream plant for twenty-five pounds of sliced dry ice. I had them cut the ice into ten-inch-long slivers about three-quarters of an inch around, wrapped the ice in heavy brown paper, and drove it back to Brookfield and the widow's jammed drill point. It's all hard-water country here, and the crimped-pipe points they drive down for wells get sealed with calcium scales if you wait enough years, and the pressure falls, the people call, they worry about having to drill new wells and how much it will cost and when they can flush the toilets again. They worry how long they'll have to wait.

I went in the cellar door without telling her I was there, disconnected the elbow joint, went back out for the ice, and when I had carried the second bundle in, she was standing by her silent well in the damp of her basement, surrounded by furniture draped in plastic sheets, firewood stacked, cardboard boxes of web-crusted Mason jars, the growing heaps of whatever in her life she couldn't use.

She was small and white and dressed in sweaters and a thin green housecoat. She said, "Whatever do you mean to do?" Her hands were folded across her little chest, and she rubbed her gnarled throat. "Is my well dead?"

"No, ma'am. I'd like you to go upstairs while I do my small miracle here. Because I'd like you not to worry. Won't you go upstairs?"

She said, "I live alone—"

I said, "You don't have to worry."

"I don't know what to do about—this kind of thing. It gets more and more of a problem—this—all this." She waved her hand at what she lived in and then hung her hands at her sides.

I said, "You go on up and watch the television. I'm going to fix it up. I'll do a little fixing here and come back tonight and hook her up again, and you be ready to make me my after-dinner coffee when I come back. You'll have water enough to do it with."

"Just go back upstairs?" she said.

"You go on up while I make it good. And I don't want you worrying."

"All right, then," she said, "I'll go back up. I get awfully upset now. When these—things. These—I don't know what to do anymore." She looked at me like something that was new. Then she said, "I knew your father, I think. Was he big like you?"

"You know it," I said. "Bigger. Didn't he court you one time?"

"I think everybody must have courted me one time."

"You were frisky," I said.

"Not like now," she said. Her lips were white on her white face, the flesh looked like flower petals. Pinch them and they crumble, wet dust.

"Don't you feel so good now?"

"I mean kids now."

"Oh?"

"They have a different notion of frisky now."

"Yes they do," I said. "I guess they do."

"But I don't feel so good," she said. "This. Things like this. I wish they wouldn't happen. Now. I'm very old."

I said, "It keeps on coming, doesn't it?"

"I can hear it come. When the well stopped, I thought it was a sign. When you get like me, you can hear it come."

I said, "Now listen: You go up. You wrap a blanket around you and talk on the telephone or watch the tv. Because I guarantee. You knew my father. You knew my father's word. Take mine. I guarantee."

"Well, if you're guaranteeing."

I said, "That's my girl." She was past politeness so she didn't smile or come back out of herself to say good-bye. She walked to the stairs and when she started to shuffle and haul the long way up, I turned away to the well pipe, calling, "You make sure and have my coffee ready tonight. You wait and make my after-dinner coffee, hear? There'll be water for it." I waited until she went up, and it was something of a wait. She was too tired for stairs. I thought to tell Bella that it looked like the widow hadn't long.

But when she was gone, I worked. I put my ear to the pipe and heard the sounds of hollowness, the emptiness under the earth that's not quite silence—like the whisper you hear in the long-distance wires of the telephone before the relays connect. Then I opened the brown paper packages and started forcing the lengths of dry ice down into the pipe. I carried and shoved, drove the ice first with my fingers and then with a piece of copper tube, and I filled the well pipe until nothing more would go. My fingers were red, and the smoke from dry ice misted up until I stood in an underground fog. When nothing more would fit, I capped the pipe, kicked the rest of the ice down into the sump—it steamed as if she lived above a fire, as if always her house were smoldering—and I went out, drove home.

I went by the hill roads, and near Excell's farm I turned the motor off, drifted down the dirt road in neutral, watching. The deer had come down from the high hills and they were moving carefully through the fields of last year's corn stumps, grazing like cattle at dusk, too many to count. When the truck stopped I heard the rustle as they pulled the tough silk. Then I started the motor —they jumped, stiffened, watched me for a while, went back to eating: A man could come and kill them, they had so little fear—and I drove home to Bella and a tight house, long dinner, silence for most of the meal, then talk about the children while I washed the dishes and she put them away.

And then I drove back to the house that was dark except for one lighted window. The light was yellow and not strong. I turned the engine off and coasted in. I went downstairs on the tips of my toes because, I told myself, there was a sense of silence there, and I hoped she was having some rest. I uncapped the well pipe and gases blew back, a stink of the deepest cold, and then there was a sound of climbing, of filling up, and water banged to her house again. I put the funnel and hose on the mouth of the pipe and filled my jeep can, then capped the check valve, closed the pipe that delivered the water upstairs, poured

water from the jeep can through the funnel to prime
the pump, switched it on, watched the pressure needle
climb to thirty-eight pounds, opened the faucet to the upstairs pipes, and heard it gush.

I hurried to get the jeep can and hose and funnel and
tools to the truck, and I had closed the cellar door and
driven off before she made the porch to call me. I wanted
to get back to Bella and tell her what a man she was married to—who could know so well the truths of ice and
make a dead well live.

Saturday morning the pickup trucks were going to the
dump, and the men would leave off trash and hard fill,
stand at tailgates, spitting, talking, complaining, shooting
at rats or nothing, firing off, picking for scrap, and I
drove to see the professor and his catastrophe.

His house was tilted. It needed jacks. The asbestos
siding was probably all that kept the snow out. His drain-
pipes were broken, and I could see the damp spots where
water wasn't carried off but spilled to the roof of his
small porch to eat its way in and gradually soften the
house for bad winter leaks. The lawn at the side of his
drive was rutted and soft, needed gravel. The barn he
used for garage would have to be coated with creosote or
it would rot and fall. A child's bright toys lay in his yard
like litter. The cornfield behind his house went off to soft
meadow and low hills, and everything was clean and
growing behind where they lived; for the view they had,
they might as well have owned the countryside. What
they didn't own was their house.

He met me at the back steps, all puffy and breasted in
his T-shirt, face in the midst of a curly black beard, dirty
glasses over his eyes like a mask. He shook my hand as if

I were his surgeon. He asked me to have coffee, and I told him I wouldn't now. A little boy came out, and he was beautiful: blond hair and sweetly shaped head, bright brown eyes, as red from weather as his father was pale, a sturdy body with a rounded stomach you would want to cup your hand on as if it were a breast, and teeth as white as bone. He stood behind his father and circled an arm around his father's heavy thigh, put his forehead in his father's buttocks, and then peeped out at me. He said, "Is this the fixing man? Will he fix our pump?"

Samuels put his hand behind him and squeezed the boy's head. He said, "This is the plumber, Mac." He raised his eyebrows at me and smiled, and I liked the way he loved the boy and knew how the boy embarrassed him too.

I kneeled down and said, "Hey, Mac."

The boy hid his face in his father's behind.

I said, "Mac, do you play in that sandbox over there?"

His face came out and he said, very politely, "Would you like to play with me?"

I said, "I have to look at your pump, Mac."

He nodded. He was serious now. He said, "Daddy broke it last night, and we can't fix it again."

I carried my tool pack to the cellar door—the galvanized sheeting on top of it was coming loose, several nails had gone, the weather was getting behind it and would eat the wood away—and I opened it up and started down the stone steps to the inside cellar door. They came behind me, then Samuels went ahead of me, turning on lights, scuffing through the mud and puddles on his concrete floor. The pump was on the wall to the left as I came in. The converted coal furnace in front of me leaked oil where the oilfeed came in. Stone foundation cracking that was two hundred years old, vent windows shut when they should have been opened to stop the dry rot, beams with the adze scars in them powdering almost as we watched: that was his cellar—and packing cartons and scraps of wood, broken chairs, a table with no legs. There was a stink of something very bad.

I looked at the pump, breathed out, then I looked at Mac. He breathed out too. He sounded like me. I grinned at him and he grinned back.

"We're the workers," he said. "Okay? You and me will be the workers. But Daddy can't fix anymore. Mommy said so."

Samuels said, "We'll leave him alone now, Mac."

I said, "How old is he?"

Mac said, "Six years old."

Samuels said, "Three. Almost three and a half."

"And lots of boy," I said.

Mac said, "I'm a worker."

Samuels said, "All right, Mac."

Mac said, "Can't stay here? Daddy? I'm a *work*er."

Samuels said, "Would we be in the way? I'd like to learn a little about the thing if I can."

Mac shook his head and smiled at me. He said, "What are we going to do with our Daddy?"

Samuels said, "Okay, buddy."

Mac raised his brows and shrugged his little arms.

Samuels said, "Out, Mac. Into the yard. Play in the sandbox for a while." He said, "Okay? I'll call you when we need some help."

"Sure!" Mac said.

He walked up the steps, arms slanted out to balance

himself, little thighs pushing up on the steps. From outside, where we couldn't see him anymore, the boy called, "Bye and I love you," and ran away.

Samuels held his arms folded across his chest, covering his fleshy breasts. He uncrossed his arms to push his glasses up on his face when they slipped from the bridge of his flat nose. He said, "The water here—I tried to use the instruction book last night, after I talked to you. I guess I shouldn't have done that, huh?"

"Depends on what you did, Mr. Samuels." I unrolled the tool pack, got ready to work.

"I figured it wouldn't turn off on account of an air block in the pipes. The instructions mentioned that."

"Oh."

"So I unplugged the pump as you told me to, and then I drained all the water out—that's how the floor got so wet. Then it all ran into that hole over there."

"The sump."

"Oh, *that's* what a sump is. Then that motor like an outboard engine with the pipe—"

"The sump pump. The water collects in the hole and pushes the float up and the motor cuts in and pumps the water out the side of the house—over there, behind your hot-water heater."

"Oh."

"Except your sump pump isn't plugged in."

"Oh. I wondered. And I was fooling with the motor and this black ball fell off into the water."

"The float. So it wouldn't turn itself *off* if you did keep it plugged in. Don't you worry, Mr. Samuels, we'll pump her out later. Did you do anything else to the well pump?"

He pushed his glasses up and recrossed his arms. "I didn't know what else to do. I couldn't make it start again. We didn't have any water all night. There wasn't any pressure on the gauge."

"No. You have to prime it."

"Prime it?"

"I'll show you, Mr. Samuels. First, you better let me look. Right?"

"Sorry. Sorry. Do you mind if I stay here, though?" He smiled. He blushed under his whiskers. "I really have to learn something about how—this whole thing." He waved his arms around him and then covered up.

I said, "You can stay, sure. Stay."

I started to work a wrench on the heavy casing bolts, and when I'd got the motor apart from the casing, water began to run to the floor from the discharge pipe over the galvanized tank.

He said, "Should I . . ."

"Excuse me?"

"There's water coming down. Should I do anything about it?"

I said, "No, thank you. No. You just watch, thank you."

After a while the trickle slowed, and I pulled the halves apart. I took the rubber diaphragm off, put the flashlight on the motor, poked with a screwdriver, found nothing. I expected nothing. It had to be in the jet. I put the light on that and looked in and saw it, nodded, waited for him to ask.

He said, "You found it?"

"Yessir. The jet's blocked. That's what it sounded like when you called. Wouldn't let the pressure build up, so the gauge wouldn't know when to stop. It's set at forty pounds, and the block wouldn't let it up past—oh, twenty-eight or thirty, I'd say. Am I right?"

"Uh, I don't know. I don't know *any*thing about these things."

I said, "When this needle hits forty, it's what you should be getting. Forty pounds of pressure per square inch. If you'd read the gauge you'd have seen it to be about thirty, I calculate. That would've told you the whole thing."

"I thought the gauge was broken."

"They generally don't break. Generally, these things work. Usually it's something simpler than machines when you can't get water up."

He pushed his glasses and covered up, said, "God, what I don't know."

I said, "It's hard to live in a house, isn't it? But you'll learn."

"Jesus, I hope so. I don't know. I hope so. We never lived in a house before."

"What'd you live in? Apartment houses?"

"Yeah—where you call the janitor downstairs and he comes up while you're at work and you never see him. Like magic. It's just all better by the time you get home."

"Well, we'll get this better for you."

He frowned and nodded very seriously. "I'll bet you will," he said. It was a gift he gave me, a bribe.

I said, "So why don't you go on up and ask the missus for about three inches of aluminum foil. Would you do that? And a coat hanger, if you don't mind."

"Coat hanger?"

"Yessir. If you don't mind."

He walked across the floor to the wooden steps that

went upstairs above the furnace; he tried to hide the sway and bounce of his body in the way that he walked, the boy coming down the outside concrete steps as the father went up the inside ones. "Do you need any help?" the boy said.

I said, "Mac, you old helper. Hello."

"Do you need any help?"

"I had a boy like you."

"A little bit big, like me?"

"Little bit big. Except now he's almost a daddy too."

He said, "Is he *your* daddy now?"

I said, "Not yet."

"Not yet?"

"Not for a while."

"Oh. Well, then what happened to him?"

"He just got big. He grew up."

"Does he go to the college?"

"He's bigger than that, even."

Mac smiled and showed his hand, fingers held together. "*That* big? *So* big?"

"Bigger," I said.

Mac said, "That's a big boy you have."

Samuels handed me the foil and coat hanger. I rolled the foil around a cigar until it was a cylinder, and I stuck it in the well side of the nozzle. I opened the hanger and straightened her out.

Mac said, "What's he doing, Daddy?"

Samuels said, "I don't know. I don't know, Mac. Why don't you go outside? I don't know."

I said, "Mr. Samuels, I wonder if you would hold that foil firmly in there and cup your hand under it while I give her a shove."

He held. Mac watched him. I pushed at the other side

of the jet, felt it, pushed again, and it rolled down the aluminum foil to his palm: a flat wet pebble half the size of the nail on his little finger. He said, "That's it? That's all it is? This is what ruined my life for two days?"

I said, "That's all it ever takes, Mr. Samuels. It came up with the water—you have to have gravel where there's water—and it lodged in the jet, kept the pressure from building up. If it happens again, I'll put a screen in at the check valve. May never happen again. If it does, we'll know what to do, won't we?"

Samuels said, "I wonder when I'll ever know what to do around here."

I said, "You'll learn."

I fastened the halves of the pump together, then went out for my jeep can, still half full from the widow's house. I came back in and I unscrewed the pipe plug at the top of the pump and poured the water in, put the plug back on, connected the pump to the switch.

Mac jumped, then stood still, holding to his father's leg.

The pump chirred, caught on the water from the widow's well, drew, and we all watched the pressure climb to forty, heard the motor cut out, heard the water climb in the copper pipes to the rest of the house as I opened the valve.

I was putting away tools when I heard Samuels say, "Now keep away from there!" I heard the *whack* of his hand on Mac's flesh, and heard the weeping start, in the back of the boy's throat, and then the wail. Samuels said, "That's *filthy* in there—Christ knows what you've dragged up. And I *told* you not to mess with things you don't know anything about. Dammit!"

Mac wailed louder. I watched his face clench and

grow red, ugly. He put his left sleeve in his mouth and chewed on it, backed away to the stone steps, fumbled with his feet and stepped backwards up one step. "But *Dad*-dy," he said. "But *Dad*-dy." Then he stood on the steps and chewed his sleeve and cried.

Samuels said, "God, look at that."

I said, "There's that smell you've been smelling, Mr. Samuels. Mouse. He must've fallen into the sump and starved to death and rotted there. That's what you've been smelling."

"God. Mac—go up and wash your hands. Mac! Go upstairs and wash your hands. I mean *now!*"

The small brown lump of paws and tail and teeth, its stomach swollen, the rest looking almost dissolved, lay in its puddle on the floor beside the sump. The stink of its death was everywhere. The pump cut in and built the pressure up again. Mac stood on the cellar steps and cried. His father pushed his glasses up and looked at the corpse of the rotted mouse and hugged his arms around himself and looked at his son. I walked past Samuels, turned away from the weeping boy, and pushed up at the lever that the float, if he had left it there, would have released on the sump pump. Nothing happened, and I stayed where I was, waiting, until I remembered to plug the sump pump in. I pushed the lever again, its motor started, the filthy reeking water dropped, the wide black rubber pipe it passed through on the ceiling swung like something alive as all that dying passed along it and out.

I picked the mouse up by its tail after the pump had stopped and Samuels, waiting for my approval, watching my face, had pulled out the plug. I carried my tools under my arm and the jeep can in my hand. I nodded to Samuels and he was going to speak, then didn't, just nodded back. I walked past Mac on the steps, not crying anymore, but wet-faced and stunned. I bent down as I passed him. I whispered, "What shall we do with your Daddy?" and went on, not smiling.

I walked to the truck in their unkempt drive that went to the barn that would fall. I carried the corpse. I thought to get home to Bella and say how sorry I was for the sorrow I'd made and couldn't take back. I spun the dripping mouse by its tail and flung it beyond the barn into Keeper's field of corn stumps. It rose and sank from the air and was gone. I had primed the earth. It didn't need the prime.

L O N G   C A L L S

When Schiff received the assignment and had to leave town, he telephoned some people to say good-bye. They said the same. The last call was to his former wife. He said good-bye to Noah, his son, who was six. Noah put Schiff's former wife back on, but they had used their farewells up, and there was nothing to do but what they did: talked low, then disconnected.

He flew from New York to Chicago, from Chicago to a college town where a bookstore called Greenspan's didn't pay its bills. On behalf of the Brothers Vogel, the law firm that employed his former wife, Schiff was to administer the inventory and mount a kind of watch while the bankruptcy suit began. He had done worse.

His motel room was a motel room. On the damage-proof surface of the bedside table was a small keyboard that turned the TV on and off. And there were his canvas suitcases, and his old BOAC flight bag containing books and cassettes and his little recorder. And, standing exhausted at the bathroom mirror, tall and wet-eyed, bald and bearded, was Schiff: former father, former husband, former older brother, once more told to be in charge.

From the motel by rented car, through the grid of streets that surrounded the school, to Greenspan's, a sea of printed paper with a four-walled desk that was an island in the center of the store. In the island, behind the cash register, a terribly pale man with red eyelids, yellow-white hair, a joint in his mouth. From speakers on the walls, Kiki Dee crying her love for music, the bass reverberating through the spines of the books.

A short fat boy in farmer's overalls and lumber jacket carried a book to the desk. His face was red, and he snorted a laugh as he handed money to the stoned man. The albino said, "Hey, let's see, what's it say—five? *Five?* Yeah, but the book only says two. Right? That say two? You giving me five, right? So—what, you want me to make you change. Right?"

Stacks, along the floor near the walls, of old quarterlies. Unlabeled shelves along the walls, going from A in fiction to R, then lapsing into philosophy. Around the corner, on the far wall, two shelves of books about women.

A sly smile moved across the albino's face and he waggled his white eyebrows. "Okay," he said, "okay. I'll make

—I'll make you change into a Big *Mac!*" He giggled and the fat boy pushed the five-dollar bill across the counter. The albino said, "You really want me to do it, right? Aw-*right*. Here we *go*."

A young man browsing beyond the island. Boxes of bright periodicals with naked women on the covers. A wall of two books—*She Did It for Everyone* and *Bondage Boy*. In an alcove opposite the desk, film and theater books, a wall of poetry, books about homosexual love. The music changing to Sly, and a song about the danger of love and amphetamines. Schiff wiped his hands against his clothes: the dust on the wood of the store, on its books, in its air, the smell of very old salad dressing and slowly leaking natural gas.

The albino leaned over the cash register. He pushed a button with one finger, then looked at the book, at the money, at the fat blushing boy, and then pushed another button. He sat back, shifted on his stool, nodded, leaned to the register again, said, "Now we do a ze-ro. *Choong*." He pushed another key, nodded, and leaned in. "Now we do a tax thing—*choong*." He leaned back, licked his lips, and said, "Now we push this big mother over *here*," and he pushed. The bell rang, the drawer slid out, and white cards in the register window stood up to say $14.05 TX. Schiff turned back to the books.

From a gray and brown curtain in the farthest end of the alcove came a tall man with long curling uncombed black hair who wore dungarees and a work shirt and boots that banged on the floor. A filtered cigarette in the corner of his mouth made him squint and tear from the right eye. He walked to the cash register island and made change, slapped it wordlessly onto the table beside the paperback book. Turning from the fat boy, the man said to the albino in a deep voice, "You gotta build my confidence, you know? You're not making me confident you can handle the job. Understand?"

The fat boy left with his book, the music changed again, someone whose voice Schiff couldn't recognize told him to seek comfort in a woman who could hold her whiskey and care for his need. The albino climbed down through a small door in the back of the island and walked past Schiff through the curtain, and the man with the cigarette in his mouth seated himself behind the cash register. Schiff walked over to the island and stood before him as the man smoked, squinting and watering from his right eye, and reading a Des Moines paper.

"Excuse me?" Schiff said.

The man looked up, squinted at Schiff with a lizard's ungenerous eye. He waited.

Schiff said, "I'm from Vogel? In New York?"

The man looked at Schiff; one eye squinted, the other eye blinked. His mouth made no expression, simply held the cigarette in place. Then emotion grew around the long beaked nose, the high cheekbones, long jaw: a forced belligerent calm. Schiff was someone's enemy again.

The man said nothing, stepped through the back of the island, and walked in heavy boots through the curtain. A few minutes later he was back with a short, stocky man dressed in brown corduroy trousers and brown buckskin shirt whose hair was almost the color of his outfit and was artfully whorled over his head to hide the baldness. The short man squinted, but with no cigarette in his mouth, and Schiff thought at first that he smiled. He didn't. He said, loudly, against the music, "You the bankruptcy guy from New York? You here to fuck us over and sell us out?"

Schiff said, "I'm the bankruptcy guy. Hey—it's a job. All right?"

The short one said, "Eichmann said that too, Mr. Bankruptcy. Everybody who killed the Jews said that. You're just obeying your orders, right?"

The tall one nodded and spat his cigarette butt onto the floor and let the filter burn there. Schiff stepped on it. "Sure," the tall one said. "Hey, fuck you. How's that?"

The short one said, "You want to burn these books or what? You want us to make a bonfire and burn the books for you? You know how long we been serving the people in this community who love *books*?"

Schiff said, "I'm sorry I stepped on your cigarette. I thought you were finished with it."

The short one said, "That was his cigarette. *I'm* talking to you. *I'm* the one, Mr. Bankruptcy. I think I hate you, you know that?"

"Listen," Schiff said, "I'll come back tomorrow and maybe you can show me the accounts and I can start the inventory. I can check the receipts tomorrow."

"You gonna check our receipts?" the tall one said. "That's nice." His voice was deep and getting louder with rage. "You gonna give us an allowance every Friday?"

Schiff put his hands in his pockets. He moved his foot away from the cigarette butt. "Which one of you is Mr. Greenspan?" he asked them.

The short one said, "We're both Mr. Greenspan. Tough luck, huh? You gotta do us *both*."

"I don't want to do anyone," Schiff said. "I'm making money so I can pay my child-support, and I'm sorry about your store. You deserve your store. It even *looks* like you. But I'm coming back tomorrow. I'll be here. I'll be wearing my storm-trooper boots."

Schiff made his exit by walking into an iron revolving rack of paperback books. He rebounded, went out into the crowded dusk of a university town. After some errant turns, he got back to the Treetop Motel—not a tree in sight, only a bright shopping mall across a four-lane arterial highway—and, after stopping at the chicken restaurant next door, he went into his room and gnawed at wings and watched a program about radiation leaks.

Later, he filled the tub and carried in the Panasonic, put a cassette on—Schubert's *Moments Musicaux*—and slid in, wincing, under the hot water, lay still. He drew his knees up because the tub was too small and then he stretched his legs out, his feet on the wall straddling the faucets. He lay like that, uncomfortably, and then closed his eyes anyway and let the music do what it did for him—allowed him to leak away.

The next morning, the short one, still in buckskin, was sitting in the little island at Greenspan's. He ate pound cake set out on waxed paper in slices like playing cards. He wrinkled his forehead as Schiff came in, then nodded, sipped coffee from a carton, pointed to the cake. Schiff shook his head and stood before the man, waiting to see what, as occupying fascist force, Schiff could expect in the way of resistance. The music wasn't on, and that made it easier. Then the short one made it easier still. He said, "You Jewish?"

"Why?"

"You know, like the joke—you *look* Jewish."

"Okay."

"You're a Jew, right?"

"Yeah. Right. So what?"

"So I said some things about Jews and Germans yesterday. Very far out of line, all right? Easy-mouth. Everybody calls everybody a Nazi if they don't like them, right? And if they feel a little paranoid, they call themselves Jews. Right?"

Schiff nodded.

"It so happens," the man said, "that the Greenspan boys ain't Jews. We're German Lutherans, right? And you're a Jew, right? So you come in here to do what you're supposed to do—I *hate* this, I want you to know I *hate* all this—and the German calls himself a Jew and he calls the Jew a Nazi, which is, uhm"—he put the yellow cake in his mouth and chewed it into a paste which flecked his tongue as he spoke again—"anyway, *that* ain't fair. So listen. Listen: We got a lawyer here, and he's gonna try and shove this involuntary bankruptcy up this New York lawyer's nose—what's his name?"

"Vogel. The Brothers Vogel."

"They Germans or Jews?"

"Both, I think."

"Yeah? That's far out. So listen, I think maybe we'll win, but what the hell. We split for the coast, we get some warm weather and some sun, right? We change the name to something very mellow, like Joe and Gordy Sweetstuff—you like that? We open a new line of credit, which is too easy to do, and meantime you do us a free inventory."

His face looked the same as it had the day before, when he'd squinted against no smoke and hated Schiff for a Jew-killer. Schiff nodded at the man and said it was his pleasure.

"I don't know what the hell we can *do* with an inventory," the man said. "We got a mess here. When you get done, we'll have a mess except with numbers attached to it. You know? Now listen, go ahead. Just don't talk to my brother too much. Joseph? Joe, he's got a hair up his ass about you. He's not a polite guy. No, you're gonna find out he's a hot-shit *person*. I mean, that aspect's cool. But his manners really suck. It's a defense mechanism." Greenspan smiled and his eyes crinkled again. Schiff held his hand out between them, as a barrier, and Greenspan reached out of his island and put a cold dry little hand in Schiff's and squeezed back.

That was Schiff's first day on the job. Gordy, the shorter brother, gave him a clipboard and a pad of legal paper and a brown bag filled with invoices dating back several months. Schiff borrowed a felt-tip pen from him and began to compare inventory to actual stock. He soon gave up, since it was clear that the invoices were incomplete. He called New York, collect, asked a junior partner at the Brothers Vogel—she was Schiff's former wife—to send their records of billings to Greenspan's, and then Schiff started to count stock, listing by category—fiction, poetry, philosophy, and so on—because it was easy to do. He listed within those categories by author or editor alphabetically. Eudora Welty was on the third shelf from the bottom near the door at the front of the store—two Modern Library *Selected Stories*. An hour later Schiff found Welty's *The Robber Bridegroom* next to the pornographic paperbacks on an unstained wooden shelf on the front of which, in pencil, was printed MARRIAGE. Schiff decided he'd find Welty's *Losing Battles* in the section on war; but when Schiff could not find such a section, Gordy proudly told him that he and Joe didn't believe in war.

Schiff worked, and Gordy turned the radio up louder. Having decided to do the alphabet at random, Schiff was at the Zs when Joe came in, about 11:45. Joe Greenspan wore the same clothes and he wore his cigarette the same way, and instead of talking to his brother or to Schiff, he stood at the door and stared at Schiff as he worked. Schiff waited for the man to speak. He didn't. He stared at Schiff and rubbed his flat belly and slowly pushed his palm through the air, in Schiff's direction and down, dismissing him from the earth. Then Joe walked through to the back room, came out with a khaki book bag, and left. Gordy Greenspan smiled what might have been his smile. Schiff listened to Judy Collins sing a song about cooking with honey.

After lunch the albino kid, not stoned, came in and Gordy left, saying he might not come back for the weekend, and if Joe didn't return the albino was to lock up.

Schiff said, "Gordy, I think I'm supposed to have a key."

Gordy smiled his possible smile and bounced on the balls of his little feet. "You're a pistol," he said. He smiled more broadly and wiped his mouth as if he still were eating. "Okay. In the back, back there. One of you guys lock up if we're gone till Monday. I don't care if you close it early, late, whatever. Everybody take care of everything, right?"

And after Gordy Greenspan had left and the albino had settled down—the register drawer open so he didn't have to solve the mysteries of the keyboard to make change—the sour spice smell of marijuana now settling onto the dust and the hard surface of the music, Schiff went into the alcove and through the curtain into the back room.

There was an aluminum folding cot on one wall, and photographs were pasted everywhere—every poet Schiff had heard of, and some fiction writers, and people who had written about the release of psychic energy and sexual tension. The wall at the back was taken up by a soot-streaked stove and a small refrigerator. Here the smell of gas was violent and threatening. A large carton on the floor in front of the cot held foreign magazines that specialized in vulvas, and on top of the magazines was a length of chain to which were attached several keys. One had a piece of tape on it labeled STORE, and Schiff removed it and went back into the shop to tell the albino he was leaving.

After lunch in a bar crowded with students, Schiff grew tired of thinking he was old, so he went back to the car and drove to the motel. He watched two giants punch themselves into exhaustion. He watched a program about nature. He watched news: Rath's reported hogs up, and beans appeared to be holding their own. First Avenue in Cedar Rapids was closed by an explosive fire. The President was confident. Schiff went out for hamburgers. He returned to watch a film about American Indian potters and then a longer film about John Wayne's triumph over other American Indians. News came on at ten o'clock in the Midwest, while the people Schiff knew in New York were listening to blues piano at the Cookery, or were in a bedroom being useful to one another.

He went to bed after putting a cassette of Boccherini on the machine. It began with the Quintet No. 2 in C Major for guitar and strings, and Schiff fell into it and through it at once, floated into Gordy Greenspan, his brother, the dust in the store and the crazy listings. Schiff thought of how, when he was married, he would hide within the cycles of their days, silently washing dishes, or coming back from a free-lance assignment, or bathing their child, or sitting with the *Times*. He would not speak and still would not, and soon he would smell shampoo and hear the sounds of cloth against her skin, which meant that the day was over again. And still he would employ the coldest language only, the vocabulary of crossed legs or of scratchings at the neck. Or the sigh of wind inside the body that arrives outside as if from a great distance. And then the baby would murmur in its room, an innocent sound without meaning or need, and Schiff would be up from the chair and chattering—*found*—and would be surprised that no one in that apartment wanted his company or wished to praise his attentions to the very young. He slept alone such nights.

The tape recorder clicked to a halt, and he reached in darkness to turn the cassette onto its other side for the Quintet in E. The music marched and he went with it, past his wife and son, thinking of his brother, and here he goes, a guerrilla stealing into his brother's room more than thirty years ago. He slides the door of his closet back on its silent track, stands among the innocent smells of small shirts and trousers, closes himself in, and waits. Here comes his brother, seven years younger than Schiff, underweight, serious, awed by his older brother's height and heft, bewildered by his lack of love or comprehension of a little brother's needs. Schiff waits until it is absolutely time. He slowly slides the door wide and makes no sound. He waits. The little brother's body moves beneath the secret of Schiff's presence. Still silent, his face drawn tight to hide his teeth, a gangster's mask, Schiff is waiting until the little brother finally *knows* he's there. He turns to see the stranger's face on the edge of his life, and he weeps. Schiff smiles with his mouth open wide.

We hope you have enjoyed this recording, said no one in an official voice, *which has been programmed to reduce program interruption for your continuous listening pleas-*

ure. Then there was silence as the empty length of tape, left for his continuous listening pleasure, moved on, then halted with a click. Schiff was sitting in bed and feeling his chest pound, was wiping at his mouth, making himself understand that there was no tape left for more music.

On Sunday he went in for a while and worked at Greenspan's, enjoying the job. He was through M and almost finished with L. He did another couple of titles and then, carrying the clipboard with him, turning off the few lights he'd been using, went into the dark cold gassy back room. It was like being underground, surrounded by stone and pools of black icy water. Lichen on the walls. Tiny white things moving slowly under rocks. He turned on a desk lamp attached to a metal cabinet above the stove. Lay on the cot in intense light. Let his legs go limp. Carried a wad of glossy magazines onto his chest and read them. Looked at thighs and crotches and great soft breasts with irritated nipples. And soon he was massaging his groin. And soon his fly was open. And soon, slowly, with lazy pleasure and no mind, he was holding and stroking and rasping himself. And soon, before a two-page photo of a fat girl sucking her own glistening finger as her membranes gleamed at him, Schiff released his sperm in gusts across his knees to the floor and the tops of his shoes. He slowly, sweatily wiped himself, and then his shoes, with a soiled blanket. He waited in half sleep until he was soft. He went back to the hotel and watched Julius Erving fly through the Chicago Bulls like a giant brown bird, again and again, to slam the ball through the hoop in vengeance for unnamed offenses.

On Monday Schiff worked. The usual flow of cus-

tomers and the usual music. Gordy stayed away and Joe
sat at the island, drinking coffee and smoking cigarettes
which he held in his mouth except when he drank. He
looked at Schiff with scorn and Schiff tried not to look
back. After lunch, when the albino hadn't come in, Joe
returned from the back room, smelling of canned ravioli,
and stood at Schiff's side, too close, while Schiff worked.
He said, "Hey. Hey. Shithead, hey. You know what we're
tryin' to *do* in here?"

Schiff didn't turn around. He said, "No."

Joe said, "Yeah. That don't surprise me, you know
that?"

Schiff said, "Right. Right, Joe."

"You're *humoring* me? Hey! *You're* humoring
me?"

Schiff clipped the sheets tighter into the clipboard and
put the pen in his pocket and said, "Bye, Joe. Have a nice
night."

"That might've been your last chance, stupid."

But Schiff went past him and out.

That night, in the motel room and in darkness, a thousand miles from home but really farther, thinking of the
people he had told good-bye, Schiff heard Joe at the door.
Joe slapped it, then thumped hard, calling, "Hey! Hey,
Bankruptcy! You wanna smoke some dope? You wanna
make peace?"

Schiff turned on the TV set but kept the sound off.

Joe called, "Yeah, okay. But I think this was the last
chance, you know?"

Schiff watched a rerun of *Star Trek* in darkness and
silence, and after a while Joe went away. Schiff continued
to watch the space ship's crewmen disappear from their

craft into tingling dotted lines, then reappear, filling their outlines again, in a barren world where there were awful creatures who meant the crewmen no good.

He was awakened again, he didn't know how much later, but he had seen American bombers and rippling flags on three channels before he'd fallen asleep. He seized the phone, a ripe new layer of sweat over his body—shins even and even the insides of his forearms—and he tried to sound calm, as if he were being graded for courage. He accepted the long-distance call, acknowledging who he was and then saying hello to his former wife.

He asked if Noah was all right. She assured him Noah was fine. She asked after his inventory work. He said fine. But then they got to business because she wanted to. He didn't care yet; he still savored Noah's safety. She had gone to check his mail, she said. He said nothing. She had thought that burglars shouldn't have clues—uncollected mail was a clue for crooks, she told him, in her business tones—and there was the Dartmouth alumni magazine. Reading it to see if his name was mentioned, she had found no catalog of his recent minor accomplishments. But she had seen his brother's name listed. With appropriate sorrow expressed by the class of '64. He was *dead*, she told Schiff. The line was silent for seconds. Then: Why hadn't Schiff *told* her? Had he known? Was it true? What would he *do*?

Schiff said that they had grown so estranged, his brother would, Schiff thought, neglect to tell him of his death.

She didn't think Schiff was funny. She wanted to know how Schiff felt.

Schiff didn't know. Then he did: "I feel like an orphan," he said. "Cheated. The bastard."

He thanked her and told her he would be in touch.

Sure, she said, wouldn't he just.

"Noah's all right?" he asked again.

She said, "He doesn't know."

"It wouldn't make any difference, I guess. I'll call you."

She said, "You won't call me back. You never call me back. You don't know *how* to call me back."

They hung up.

Schiff sat on the bed, then went to his flight bag for his notebook of names and addresses. He set out the clipboard of inventoried titles, flipped back pages of the long legal pad until he had a clean sheet ready and the clipboard set by the phone. He dialed for an outside line, reached an operator, and started to call across the country, to verify his brother's dying.

First his brother's number in San Diego. No answer.

Then the San Diego night supervisor. Confirmation that the number worked. Schiff asked how long it would take to disconnect a dead man's phone. The operator said probably a month or three weeks after the last bill was due.

Then Schiff's local operator said, "Are you all right, honey?" When he told her why he wasn't, she said, "Make sure you're sitting down. Are you sitting down?"

Schiff's operator called the central police station in San Diego. Giving his brother's address, she learned which local station might have responded if Schiff's brother had fallen over from a charge of drugs too bright and hard for his body, or been stabbed on the sidewalk near his loft. She worked through exchanges and raised a sergeant near his brother's address. Schiff told the sergeant how he'd learned of his brother's death, and when he thought it might have taken place. Schiff told the sergeant he was guessing. The sergeant sighed into the phone. Schiff gave him the name and address and the sergeant went away to check, returned with no information, told Schiff he would send a car to the loft, instructed him to call back in half an hour. Meanwhile, the sergeant said, did Schiff want to make more calls? Schiff did, and the sergeant gave him the name of the hospital into whose emergency room his brother might have been brought. "If he was mugged, you know, or DOA," the sergeant said.

Schiff said, "That means dead on arrival?"

So his operator, still on the line, obtained and called the number for Metropolitan Hospital's emergency room. Schiff spoke to a nurse who gave him over to an orderly who, with great calmness and almost tender care, went back through records, finding no reference to Schiff's brother. Schiff thought of himself in the closet in his brother's room, sliding the door back slowly, no expression on his face.

"But that doesn't mean he didn't die," the orderly said. "It just means he didn't die *here*. He might have died on the street and been brought into the medical examiner's office DOA."

"That means dead on arrival," Schiff said. "Am I right?"

The orderly gave Schiff the medical examiner's number—the operator cut in to say, "I have that, sir"—and they went again through the dancing high-sung notes of the long-distance wire.

A man in the medical examiner's office was bored by Schiff's story, though not cruel—he was only conducting his business. He went back through records, farther back, then said Schiff's name aloud and spelled it to Schiff.

Schiff said, "Yes." The man spelled it again. Schiff said,
"Yes."

Then the man said, "No, this one's too young. Your
brother's thirty-two? No. This one's twenty-eight."

"It's pretty close, though," Schiff said.

"Your brother a Negro?"

He wouldn't tell me if he was.

Or: *Not the last time I looked, but that was so long
ago.*

Or: *Quite possibly, by now.*

Schiff said, "No, I have a Caucasian brother."

"You're clear as far as I can see. This guy was
black."

"Thank you," Schiff said.

"Thank *him*," the man said.

Schiff thought of his wife on the floor of their living
room—his former wife—with Noah leaning against her
drawn-up knees, her hand on his hair and the back of
his neck, reading him the story, again, of Arthur Cluck,
and of how Arthur Cluck disappeared from his loving
mother hen, and how Ralph the Owl, barnyard detective,
found Arthur Cluck and brought him home. Schiff's wife's
low voice, telling about losses.

His operator asked if he was all right, and Schiff told
her he was, then gave her numbers: the art school where
his brother had taught—still taught? once taught?—part-
time; the name of his brother's chairman; the number of
a woman whom his brother had claimed once to love.
Schiff's toes felt cold on the motel carpet, and, clamping
the phone to his shoulder with his head, he wrapped a
blanket around his body. He felt tender toward himself.

The chairman did not answer. The woman wasn't
home and the man who answered didn't know when she

would be; the man said he didn't care. The operator said this was important. The man said he still didn't care. The watchman at the art school said no one was there and Schiff should *know* that no one was there.

So Schiff thanked the operator, told her how fine she'd been, told her of his gratitude—his voice began to wobble, then—and said he'd try the numbers later on. He hung up.

He wanted food. He had to have food, so he dressed and went down the corridor to the vending machines. With all his change he bought four Mars Bars, went back to sit on the bed, dropping wrappers on the carpet, filling himself with sweetness. He lay on the bed, turned on the remote-control switch, worked through the channels, found glaring whiteness and the high hum of empty air, turned the set off, closed his eyes. He didn't sleep, but lay there, and lay there, and then he rolled and sat up, planted his feet on the carpet again. He said to the room, "My brother's dead. My brother is dead. My brother is dead."

He answered: "You should have thought of that before." But he didn't understand what he meant. He picked up the phone and dialed the number in San Diego at four in the morning and listened to the telephone ring.

Nothing. Schiff hung up. The phone rang, and Schiff ripped it from the cradle: "Hello? *Hello?*"

"This is the operator, honey. Can I get any more numbers for you? Did you find anything out?"

Schiff said, "Oh. Oh. You're wonderful, you know that?" He was crying, but he tried to sound businesslike, and said, "Thank you, no thank you, it'll be fine, thank you very much, thank you."

And then the phone did not ring, and he watched it,

and then dialed to San Diego again, and listened to it ring for no one in California, and then Schiff hung up to wait.

He rewound the Boccherini, and let it play.

He dialed the number in San Diego.

His brother answered at once: "Yeah?"

"Hey," Schiff said, tightening his throat and eyes. "Hey, it's me."

There was a new silence—the music of estrangement—and then his brother said, "Hey, hey, man. What's up?" What's up: What is the business we have to transact?

"I heard you were dead," Schiff said.

"Who told you that? Are they right?" Schiff's brother giggled, then was silent, then barked a laugh, and said "Oh, wow. Oh, *wow*. What a mess. What a—"

"Me?" Schiff said, with the innocence of begged love.

"I was getting those, you know, alumni letters? You know. We need a hundred million dollars by next week, so please send all your money? I got so goddamn tired of getting all that junk—"

"*You* did it?"

"What?"

"No, tell me, you go ahead."

"I wrote them this letter from my widow, see? I told them I died—my husband, who was me. I told them it really got me upset—the widow—to keep getting these letters to him. *Me*. Him. You know?"

Schiff tried to whistle and couldn't. "Got it. Right. Right. Listen—I made about fifty dollars' worth of calls. I believed it. See, I thought you were *dead*. I called the cops near you, and—Jesus! I forgot to call the cops back!"

"Maybe you didn't miss me as much as you thought."

"No," Schiff said, "I was calling hospitals and emergency rooms and the medical examiner to find out if you got DOA'd, that's dead on arrival. I called your chairman. I called all your friends I ever heard of."

"You really tracked me down, huh?"

Schiff's brother's voice sounded to Schiff like Schiff's.

His brother said, "Well, you know what to do in emergencies at least, don't you?"

"Yeah, I guess I'm good at that."

They let the line stay silent for a long time.

"I hope you see the humor in all this," his brother said.

"Well."

"It sounds like you're having a hard time seeing the humor in all this."

Schiff held onto the receiver with both hands and heard their silence.

"Well," Schiff said, his voice pitching. "Well, maybe I will. Maybe next week or something. I believed it."

Their silence again, and then, as if he'd suddenly got very busy, Schiff's brother said, "Well, I tell you what. Why don't you drop me a postcard or something when you see how all this is kind of funny. All right? How's that?"

Schiff stood up, and all his words for anger and apology came to the back of his teeth and died there. He swallowed them. He said, "All right. All right. All right. I'm glad you're alive." He waited to say something better for himself, and maybe even for his brother, but his brother disconnected and Schiff put his phone down too.

The Boccherini went on for a little while, and then the room was still. Schiff sat on the bed, cross-legged, cold. He picked up the telephone and dialed his wife's

number, but hung up. He walked around the room, lay
down in bed, slept.

He woke, went back to sleep, woke an hour later in
light and told himself what had happened. He drove
downtown to work.

Melissa Manchester sang "Midnight Blue." Joe sat in the
island, his cigarette in place, his hands in his lap, and anger,
as ever, on his face. The smell of gas was harsher this
morning, and there seemed to be more magazines piled
in the dirty-books section, and a box of what looked like
old bedclothes. Schiff thought of his recently invested
sperm. Gordy came from the back room, crinkled his
face in what might have been a smile, and said, "Okay."

Joe nodded back. Gordy went out of the store and
Joe beckoned Schiff to the island. Schiff went, carrying
the clipboard. "I came to see you, Bankruptcy."

"I heard you, Joe. I was trying to stay alone last night.
And some things came up. Maybe I would have called
you, but some things came up."

"I knew you were there." He squinted through his
smoke. Schiff wiped at his face because the gas smell
was heavier. "That was it, pal, last night. You wouldn't've
called me."

Schiff said, "No." He turned around and went to the
section of poetry books in the alcove near the curtain.
The gas was dense there and Schiff turned to say so, but
Joe was gone. Schiff went back to the island and saw that
the store was empty. The sign that hung in the glass door
said OPEN. But that was the side facing Schiff. He went to
the alcove and through the curtain and smelled the gas
leaking into the store from the stove. He heard it hiss

from all four open unlit burners, and from the oven, a great black mouth that gaped at his own.

He shut the burners off and went back to the far side of the shop where dirty smoke made Schiff sneeze in shrieks. The rags that Joe had lit before leaving had caught onto some silky sex magazines, and Schiff saw the filter of Joe's cigarette nested in burning pages. He kicked the box along the floor before it could light a shelf of books and, as the Greenspans had planned, build up heat enough to ignite the leaking gas and blow the books away, their debts away, and their bankruptcy caretaker too.

The flames and black smoke jumped back at him as Schiff shoved the box with his feet. He couldn't see through the smoke, so he had to dance around the burning box and then back behind it once he'd set his course. He unlocked the front door and, holding it open, kicked the box as far into the street as he could. A woman walking past with her child screamed and pulled the child out of the way. A man in a peacoat walked over to inspect the flames.

"Hey!" Schiff shouted. "Hey! *Call* someone!"

He was dizzy with smoke or excitement, and his legs tingled. He went back to the other burning magazines and kicked them away from the wall, then danced on them —nipples and pubic mounds, rounded offering mouths— until Schiff's heavy feet had put the fires out. And then, gagging, moving his legs with difficulty, Schiff ran into the back room and put the clipboard under his arm, grabbed his parka, and went coughing into the street.

Schiff heard sirens. His skin simmered with excitement. He went to his knees, an altar boy. He felt a hard push or punch at his back, and he went all the way down.

While he still was trying to ask who had attacked him, and why, there were hands on him, pulling at his legs, his belt, hands holding him and tearing his trousers away. The man in the peacoat held Schiff's trousers up for Schiff to see—they were charred below the knees, and on one thigh an oval hole burned steadily at the edges, growing wider as Schiff watched.

He let his head drop back. Someone's hand cushioned it. He moaned. He let the clipboard fall away. Schiff discovered that he wept. He laughed and then he started weeping again, daintily touching his injured thigh. Above him, the man who had torn off his trousers flinched from Schiff's eyes.

Schiff said, "I have to make a call."

The man said, "What?"

"It *hurts*! I have to make a call."

"Wait a second, will you? Will you wait? First get fixed up. *Then* you make your call, for chrissakes. Don't be a nuisance right away. Lie down and wait, for chrissakes."

Schiff said, "No—"

The man turned away.

Schiff heard himself snorting, half-naked on the sidewalk. He touched at his burns. The klaxons were close. Now he had to call his wife back, now he had to. He had to tell her how he knew what to do now—how to save things, how to place long calls—in emergencies at least.

COMPANY

Every day did not start with Vince awake that early, dressing in the dark, moving with whispery sounds down the stairs and through the kitchen, out into the autumn morning while groundfog lay on the milkweed burst open and on the stumps of harvested corn. But enough of them did.

I went to the bedroom window to watch him hunt in a business suit.

He moved with his feet lost in the slowly stirring fog, moving slowly himself with the rifle held across his body and his shoulders stiff. Then he stopped in a frozen watch for woodchucks. His stillness made the fog look faster as it blew across our field behind the barn. Vince stood. He waited for something to shoot. I went back to the bed and lay beneath our covers again. I heard the bolt click. I heard the unemphatic shot, and then the second one, and after a while his feet on the porch, and soon the rush of water, the rattle of the pot on top of the stove, and later his feet again, and the car starting up as he left for work an hour before he had to.

And later, with sun on the windows and the house warming up, I said to Sammy, my brother-in-law, "Well, listen, turkey, you got a Master of Fine Arts, you can master a Maytag washing machine, right?" I was smoking filtered cigarettes that tasted like cardboard because the brand I'd smoked the day before had tasted like fingernails. I wanted a long nasty Pall Mall, and I hadn't smoked one in a week—my cough wasn't better, and neither was my mood. I kept remembering something from Friday night TV when I was a kid, a mellow deep voice from the little round Dumont flickering blue in the dark room: "Fine tobacco is its own best filter. Pall Mall's extra length filters the smoke. And makes it . . . mild." When Sammy was standing up, I had an extra length on him, about an inch and a half. Now he was sitting at the kitchen table while I stood, so I was longer still, but nothing was making me mild.

He rubbed his big bald head and lit one of my cigarettes and said, "Oh, wow, Nina, Jesus—you sound like you been out on the *street*."

"No," I said. "I watched TV last night, late. It was the good guys against the turkeys. And I'm a good guy. I don't want to do your laundry."

He got up to pour more coffee and to look into the

black iron skillet, which still was empty. As he stood, it was like looking at Vince's near twin—or a drawing someone had made of Vince, botching the way the hair grew on the neck, the size of the eyes, the weight of the upper lip. But Sammy was here. Vince had gone early again, and Sammy had stayed, sleeping beside his new cause while I got Jean into her dress and out to the school bus.

Sammy and the cause had come the night before, on a Trailways bus, and Vince had gone in the Saab to fetch them. On the way home the Saab had thrown a fan belt— nothing important, Vince said—and Sammy insisted we needed a better car. Vince, smiling and shaggy and embarrassed, had told him we couldn't afford one. So Sammy had instructed Vince where we needed to allocate our resources—not in my little kiln, he said, or the loom, or the useless wooden icebox we'd bought for me to re- finish, or the Hoosier cabinet with its flour bin and tin counter. Sammy said we ought to get involved with engines of freedom and means of flight, not structures of bulk that pinned us down.

Vince had looked away from me during the lecture. Sammy's cause had looked away from Sammy and me and Vince. According to Sammy, she wasn't into posses- sions and comforts right then. She was into survival, he'd told us officially. When he'd reported that, I'd gotten Jean into the tub, and Vince into the dishes, and my fingernail into my mouth—mostly to keep myself from telling them both to report to the front desk and check *out.*

So when Sammy, a not infrequently published poet, brought down a wad of laundry in the morning—gray- brown jockey shorts, a weathered flannel shirt, a blue brassiere, and blue bikini panties—I decided not only to try another brand of filtered cigarettes, but to make a little statement: turkey, MFA, washing machine.

Oh, wow, Jesus, streets, etc.

And now Sammy was drinking his second cup of coffee, and smoking a second cigarette—tapping the ashes into the saucer, I noted for the warrant of particulars I thought of posting on their headboard with a four-inch paring knife—and he was jiggling his right knee and tapping his fingers on the kitchen table and pursing his lips and giving me, in short, his imitation of a man who was set upon by harridans.

"You're not," I told him.

"Huh?"

"You're not set upon, and I'm not a harridan."

"What?"

"Never mind. Do you want some eggs?"

The cause was named Charlotte, and he called her—what else? what, in the age of elegant survival, else?—Charlie. Charlie came into the kitchen looking sullen and delicious, small in loose white slacks and no shoes and one of Sammy's dirty work shirts, and clearly the owner of only one brassiere, currently on the floor before my Maytag. She was maybe twenty and looked less. I am thirty-four. She made me feel forty. She made me feel fat. She made me embarrassed. I made them four eggs over and English muffins.

Sammy held her hand while they drank their orange juice, and he smoothed her curly blond hair. It sprang up curly again. Mine lay flat and thin, and I couldn't help pushing at it. Charlie smiled—her teeth were crooked and white—and she said, in a soft low voice, "I wish my hair was straight, Nina."

At which point I was supposed to say, "I wish mine

was curly like yours, Charlie." So I did. I also broke a coffee cup, and they watched me put the shards in the trash.

They ate their eggs, I washed the dishes from Jean and me, and Vince's coffee cup, and Sammy told Charlie how beautiful it was where we were, ninety miles from Philadelphia, outside Allentown, on the fringe of Pennsylvania's Amish country. Sammy had known the Amish folk from Iowa, where he got his degree in poetry writing. He instructed us in their quaint customs, and told how, near Iowa City, they still refused to send their children to public schools. "So the school board decides it's the law, and they *have* to go to school. We're out there in the boonies, a few of us, just taking a walk and like looking around, and there's this kind of hamlet, little wooden houses and big barns, all Amish people, and suddenly three giant yellow school buses pull up, all the brakes go on at the same time. *Grown-ups* get out of the buses, guys with beer gut and heavy shoes, and all of a sudden all the doors in all the little houses open at the same *second*. See, they're sending the sheriffs or somebody to get the kids into school. The Amish people are waiting for them. All of the doors open up and all of the kids take off into the fields, all this green high stuff, big as the kids, and they keep going, scared shitless and running like a bitch. We could see the trails they made. Pretty soon, though, the trails closed off, the grass kind of relaxed back to where it was, and that's that. The kids keep still, the sheriffs are standing there, up to their stomachs and chests in corn and weeds and all kinds of shit, and nothing moves except the wind. It goes through the tops of everything, so even if the kids *did* move, you couldn't've told the kids from the wind. The sheriffs keep standing there, talking to each other in these low staticky voices on their walkie-talkies, mostly saying 'Over' and 'Roger,' with their voices falling away at the ends of the words, and the parents are standing in the doorways—a mother and a father in every doorway, just looking, with their really white faces and their really black clothes. And after half an hour of looking stupid, the sheriffs get back in their school buses really slow and pissed off, and all of the brakes go at the same time, and they drive back into town. Beautiful. So we go down to talk to the parents and tell them how really fine it was. They see us coming, and they call out something to the kids, and nothing moves in the field except the wind, and all the doors slam closed. That is strong suspicion," Sammy said, looking at me as I turned where I stood at the sink.

I listened for more, but he didn't want to push it, and he probably was too tangled in his parable to figure out what he wanted me to learn. The sun was hot by now on our hill and the sumac losing its first bright red, the maples coming on in turn, orange and scarlet, and I decided to work outside. There was an old pine rocker I wanted to strip, so I boiled water and carried out washing soda and a heavy brush. I told them to drink more coffee and stay inside, but they followed me. Sammy said to Charlie, "You might want to learn some of this, you know?"

Near the garden, with tomato vines withered from the first frost and the brussels sprout leaves blue-green in the sun, I mixed boiling water with washing soda and scrubbed the mixture onto the dark-stained chair, rinsing with the hose, then scouring more hot water on. A little at a time, the old wood came up through the film of brown varnish. First it showed dark orange and then, when it was rinsed, and as the sun worked, it turned deep pink, then lighter pink, and then it was wood.

Charlie and Sammy sat on the back-porch steps, watching me. Sammy smoked my cigarettes. Charlie smoothed the legs of her slacks and watched her hands. Sammy said, "It looks like newborn skin."

I turned the hose off. I threw the brush in the steaming bucket. I said, "Hey, Sammy, keep your poetry to yourself." I reached in for the brush and scalded myself and went between them up the steps and into the house and locked myself in the bathroom. I ran cold water on my fingers and insisted on not crying. The phone rang. It rang again, and it kept ringing. When I counted fourteen and Sammy still hadn't answered it, I unlocked the door and went into the kitchen, knocking three times on the wooden wall-molding—wincing, because the knuckles were tender—so it wouldn't be the school saying something was wrong with Jean, or the troopers saying Vince had crashed the car. As I picked the receiver from its cradle on the wall, I understood that I always knocked on wood when I answered the phone.

Vince said, "You okay, hon?"

I did my imitation of "Grrrrrr" and then hiccuped my phony telephone laugh. I said, "Yup. Yup. I took so long getting here because I thought Sammy would pick it up."

"Not his line of country," Vince said, in a bad fake English voice. "Shit," he said. Which added up to: I know it's a pisser for you, and it's tough for me, but he's my *brother.*

I said, "Nah." Which meant: You're goddamn right, but he *is* your *brother.*

Vince said, "Yeah," and breathed out into the telephone —the static reminded me of the sheriffs in Iowa, talking on their radios, chasing the Amish kids into the fields—and then he said, "Listen, they want me to go to Philly for a couple of days. They figure anyone who spent a year in France looking at cathedrals is the one guy in a firm of sixty who can handle—you ready?—a parking lot outside the new Penn alumni club in Center City."

I said, "That's why you love your work."

"Yazzuh. But anyhow they said I could take you along, and we could stay there together and futz around a little on company money. You like that idea?"

"What about Jean? Remember her?"

"I thought about that. I *thought* about that. See, if we take her, then it's too much of a family thing, and the accountants wouldn't like it."

"We'll pay for her."

"No, my supervisor won't buy it. Wives are okay, kids aren't—straight company policy."

"So you're about to suggest that we leave our seven-year-old daughter, who gets the croup in wet weather, with your twenty-eight-year-old brother, who thinks he's made a commitment of serious dimensions when he buys a new shirt and consents to keep it?"

"No," Vince said, "I'm about to suggest that I have to go to Philly tomorrow alone, and I'm sorry, and maybe I should quit my job."

We let it stay silent for a while so we could make the usual private faces at the usual mutual fate, and then I said, "But how else could a serious student of architecture get a crack at parking wealthy alumni?"

"Right," he said.

"Are you pissed off, Vince?"

"Only at life and God and man's unendurable dilemma."

"Yeah, that one's a real bitch."

"Okay," he said. "I'll come home early if I can and rescue you."

"Listen," I said, "it's all right."

"Life with a twenty-eight-year-old teenager isn't always easy, huh?"

"Don't we both sound smug," I said.

"Yes."

"You think we *should* be?"

He waited, and then he said, "Why not?"

"Okay," I said. "I was wondering."

Then he said, "Love."

I said, "Love."

Sammy, behind me, said, "That my big brother?"

I didn't turn around. I said, "No, Sammy, that was the Lithuanian dwarf who's my lover. We get it off on the phone."

I faced the phone while the silence grew. Then Sammy said, "Okay. Okay. Can I use Vince's twenty-two? Just stroll the fields and murder things?"

I said, "Be careful. The bullets are in the cupboard near the flour cannister. Be careful."

He said, "Yes, Mother."

I put a dark wash in, leaving their clothes where they were on the floor, and then I did their breakfast dishes. The water hurt my hand, so I put a rubber glove on it, and I thought about Philadelphia years back, about going to dinner with Vince in Chinatown and then walking down to the river. I thought about the Show Bar near the Troc, where the strippers came in to drink boiler-makers with Frank the owner, and how when it was very late and everyone was drunk enough and stuffing themselves with his partly cooked hot dogs, Frank would show us slides in the back—his nephew on a horse, his nephew off the horse, his nephew alone, the horse alone. Vince would talk with Frank about the Eagles' losing season, or the Phillies' chances of getting a good short reliever for the bullpen, and I would talk to the strippers about their mutual funds and *their* nephews.

So I guess I was standing there, with my one safe hand in the water, when Charlie came in alone and said, "Nina, can I talk to you?"

I looked at her, and her face was made of several faces, each of them troubled differently. I took my cigarettes and lighter from the table and, dripping soapy water on the floor, said, "Why don't we go upstairs."

Charlie sat cross-legged on our bed, watching her hands smooth her slacks. I sat on the old Morris chair, leaning back, smoking, looking at the old engraving of Stonehenge behind her on the wall. It showed eighteenth-century farmers feeding huge fires in order to crack stones, so they could splinter and haul them away, giving their cattle better access to graze.

Charlie said, "Do you like having kids?" Her voice was very low, and I could hear it saying sexy things to men.

I looked more closely, but couldn't tell. "When are you due?" I said.

She closed her eyes and her head drooped on the pale thin neck. I didn't hear what she answered.

"Sweety, what'd you say?"

"Seven months, I think. About that."

"You're not seeing a doctor?"

She shook her head. Her eyes stayed closed.

"Whatever you do," I said, "you have to see a doctor. Okay? Whatever else we talk about, whatever we say, and whatever you finally decide to do about it, you see a doctor until you make your final move. All right? I'll help you find someone if you want. Do you have any money?"

She said, "He has money."

"He *does?*"

She looked up, and her eyes were wide and bright and wet—someone with a fever, or something on the run. "Oh, no," she said. "No, it isn't Sammy. Did you think it was him? No. It isn't Sammy."

I swallowed and lit another cigarette.

She said, "I know you don't like him."

"No," I said, "it isn't that."

"I know," she said. "You don't like having to think about him being generous. But he's taking care of me. We're staying together. He isn't leaving me alone."

"And the other guy is?"

"No. Not really."

"Oh. You don't want him."

"I don't want him," she said. "I don't want any of it."

"You don't want his baby, either?"

She snapped at me. Her lips actually drew back from her gums and she *was* an animal, fleeing, angry, scared. "It's *my* baby."

I wanted to say, "Your baby *too*," but I didn't. What she'd said was better than what I'd said, and anyway we both were wrong. At that moment it was *their* baby. Which meant, at that moment, nobody's baby. I heard myself telephoning Vince and saying, "Listen, if we can't go to Philly together, why don't we plan to adopt a kid?"

I rubbed at my forehead and realized that I wore a rubber glove. I put the cigarette out, and stripped the glove away, wiped my sweating sore hand on my dungarees, and lit a cigarette. I draped the glove across my lap. I said, "What are you planning to do with your baby?"

"I want to have an abortion."

I thought of a tiny white polypy person with drawn-down eyelids dying out of her into a plastic pail. I looked at her and thought that she was right. She couldn't take care of anyone. She was into survival, Sammy had said. I thought she was right. I said, "And the—the father will help you?"

"He'll pay."

She looked at me. I felt vulnerable, lying back beneath my middle-aged lap and smoking cigarettes. I sat up and said, "You don't want him to pay."

"No. I don't."

"Can Sammy help you?"

"He wants me to have the baby and marry him and we all stay together in a family."

"*Sammy* wants that?"

"Sammy loves me."

"Sammy really loves you?"

"Yes, he does."

"Is it all right if I ask you if you—"

"No," she said. "No, I don't."

"And you wouldn't consider staying with him any-way, in—"

"In a family. No."

"So you made up your mind, then."

"No. All I decided is whatever I do, I should do it alone. It's mine, the whole thing's mine, and I hate it. But all I decided is that. You don't understand me, Nina."

I lit another cigarette and coughed unprettily. When I was finished and had wiped my eyes and smeared at my nose, I said, "But, honey, what'd you want us to *talk* about?"

"You have this terrific household thing going here, and you and Vince and Jean—you know about these things. You know about kids—"

"We couldn't have any more," I said. "I had to get a lot scooped out. I can't have children anymore. So all I know about is Jean. She's plenty to know about, but I'm just one up on you by a few years is all. Charlie, I don't know that much, Charlie."

"Do you think I should have the baby?"

"Or kill it?"

"Or get an abortion. Yes."

Listen, Vince, if we can't go to Philly together and you need to carry a gun around before breakfast, why don't we plan on adopting a kid.

Listen, Charlie, carry the child and we'll pay all your bills and get you into a splendid hospital and why don't we plan on adopting your kid?

I held the rubber glove by the palm and with my other hand drew the index finger back as far as I could and snapped it. I did that again, while Charlie stared at me and waited. She looked like a child in a terrible city, lost and not speaking the language. I snapped the finger again. She got off the bed and walked out of the bedroom and very lightly down the stairs. I snapped the finger and heard the back door close.

Pretty soon there were feet on the stairs. I waited, but I knew. Sammy came in, his clothes dark with moisture and a wide sly grin on his face. It was almost Vince with that grin. He stood at the doorway, and he said, "I heated up the mixture again and I finished cleaning off that chair for you."

"Well," I said, "many thanks. Thank you. Wait—you heated that gunk in a *pot*? On the *stove*?"

"Yeah, it kind of screwed up the saucepan."

"You're an asshole, Sammy, you know that?"

He shrugged his shoulders, then nodded. He said, "Charlie told you, huh?"

"We talked about it."

I lit a cigarette, offered one to him, lit his too. Now that he was closer, he squatted beside my chair, looking up at me and making me feel old again. He said, "That's why I boiled the water, right? Like in the movies—you boil water and tear petticoats when someone has a baby."

"You're a pioneer, Sammy. Is that why you wanted Vince's gun? To get in the mood?"

"I thought I wanted to kill something," he said. "I thought maybe I could shoot a woodchuck. But I don't know what a woodchuck looks like, and I couldn't've pulled the trigger, anyway. The gun really scared me. So I cleaned off the chair."

"Sammy," I said, "where's Charlie now?"

"She went for a walk out near the barn."

"Sammy, where did you leave the gun?"

"Why are you asking me that?"

I looked at him. His eyes were enormous. They stayed that way when he stood up.

He said, "Nina, why are you asking me that?"

We heard the shot. It was very flat, there was no echo, hardly much noise to begin with, like hardwood suddenly split. Sammy turned and ran to the stairs. I ran after him. I was panting. He was too. We went out the back door and down the steps, across the yard past the garden to the barn. Charlie stood in the wide doorway. She held the .22 across her body. She was smiling. Part of the top of her ear was gone, and she was shaking. Her face was covered with sweat. She let the rifle go, and with blood streaked across her curly bright hair, she bent over and vomited onto my feet. I knelt and held onto her. She retched and bled and then Sammy started retching too. I looked over her head and her blood at my brother-in-law. I said, "Marry him, Charlie."

She heaved and panted in my arms. Sammy looked up, drooling and pale.

Charlie's voice was muffled by my skin. It asked, "Who? Which *one*?"

"Either one," I said. "Any one."

THE LESSON
OF THE
HÔTEL LOTTI

My mother's lover was always exhausted, and yet he
generated for me, and I think for her too, a sense of the
most inexhaustible gentleness, and the strong calm I
grew up thinking a prerequisite for love. He was a lawyer
with offices at the foot of Manhattan, a neighborhood he
knew intimately and talked about compellingly. The son
of Austrian immigrants, a Jew, he lectured gently on
Trinity Church and practiced maritime law, a field not
famous for its renunciations of the more vulgar bigotries.
He was the same age as my mother, fifty-five, when they
started practicing deceptions and certainly cruelties upon

his wife. And when my mother died at sixty-two, a couple of years after he did, she had suffered the most dreadful solitude, for he was necessary.

I was unplanned, unexpected, and apparently less than desirable. Born when my mother was thirty-nine, I was doubtless part of what happened not long thereafter. My father, who owned yards—a pleasure-craft boat yard, two lumberyards, and part of an undistinguished California vineyard—left my mother, and me, for a woman with inherited land in a suburb of London called Edgware. I have been there, for reasons I don't need to make clear; it looks like Flatbush Avenue in Brooklyn, though less permanent—every other house seems to be in a state of rebuilding or repair—and I never will need to go back. I grew up as much my mother's younger sister as her child. And the older I became, the more accomplished I was said to be, so my mother grew more fatigued by the world, more easily dismayed.

I have composed some recollections, for the sake of sentiment—I don't want to lose *anything* now—and so I think that I recall him standing silently at the door of our apartment on East 50th Street, late one night, as they returned from the theater. He seemed reluctant to walk farther in. I think I remember his smile: lips tightly closed (he had bad teeth), the long frown-lines from the nose to the corners of his mouth (they later became the boundaries of jowls), the pale blue eyes content but ready not to be. I think I can call him ironic, in the sense that he inspired, and dealt with, several emotions at once; he never surrendered to sarcasm. He looks larger in this possible early recollection than he was but, then, I feel smaller, when I remember him, than I am. He was nearly six feet tall, but because of his short legs he looked less large when I knew him well. His head was bald, the fringe gone chestnut and white. His face was square, his neck solid but not thick. His nose was wide without being bulbous. He was a slender man with a broad chest and strong shoulders, and he dressed in dark expensive suits. His voice was deep; it could snap and yap and snarl, or it could rumble soothingly as he spoke of what he loved, and nearly always when he talked to me it was with a graveled gentleness I have heard no other man use.

For years, my mother spoke of "my attorney," or "my legal adviser," or, as I grew older, "our lawyer." Then it became "Leonard Marcus says" and then "Leonard." He came to my graduation from the Brearley School, and I introduced him as "my Uncle Leonard," although my mother had never called him that. The night of my graduation, the three of us had dinner at the Russian Tea Room and went to a revival of *Our American Friend*. I thereafter left for a party with classmates, and when I came home early because I had decided to age quickly by finding myself bored with my intimate companions of four years, I found my mother waiting in the living room for a talk.

For a talk: a separate category in our lives, signaled by a silver drinks tray on the coffee table, a round stone ashtray, and a packet of Player's cigarettes, which my mother had come more and more to smoke too many of —perhaps to remind her, in distress, of the England my father had fled to. The sailor on the packet had blue eyes, and on his hatband was the word HERO.

She wore a long challis housecoat and no slippers, and sat in a corner of the sofa with a plaid blanket held across her lap; I had bought the blanket for her in England during my pointless pilgrimage there the summer before. We greeted each other matter-of-factly, per our tacit agreement not to become hysterical until it was clearly a necessity, and for a few minutes we discussed how remarkably mature I had become, in contrast to my friends, in the course of a single evening. She made herself a drink—Calvados and soda with ice—and I made my own sophisticated bourbon and ginger ale. She lit a Player's Navy Cut, hissed smoke out at me, and then caught her breath as I took a package of Kools from my bag and lit up too.

"Well, well," she said.

I shrugged.

"About Leonard," she said.

"Where is he?"

"Leonard's at home with his wife."

I puffed as if the cigarette were a pipe. My face beat hot, and I'm sure I felt the same sense of landslide felt by children who in their teens are asked, "Did you ever think you might be adopted, darling?" But I managed to say, as if it weren't the second commencement of the day, "Gee, I didn't know he was married, Anya."

"Leonard is a married man," my mother said, nodding, and with a note of pride in her voice—a sound I would hear again when I came home from Vassar to discuss with her my first and unspectacular coupling, with a boy from Union College.

"Has he been married—uh—all the time?"

My mother nodded and drank some brandy, said across the rim of her glass, "We have always been having an *affaire*." Her French was manifest and overaccented; she was an educated woman, and never untheatrical. "He is not your uncle, darling."

"Well, that's all right, Anya."

"Susu," she said.

"Anya, would you mind very much calling me Suzanne?" I said.

So I was Suzanne, and he was not Uncle Leonard, nor simply our attorney, Leonard Marcus. And shortly, we were a domestic routine. Once the declaration had been made, it wasn't mentioned again—by me, because I was in awe of an *affaire* conducted by a woman with varicose veins who was my humdrum, pretty, and flustered mother; by her, because I tried very hard that summer to rarely be home.

I worked at the neighborhood Gristede's during the day, and at night I kept moving—the evening jazz concerts at the Museum of Modern Art, or Shakespeare in the Park, or films at the Thalia, or shopping for frights on Eighth Street in the Village, or posed and dramaturgical dates ending with kisses on the Staten Island ferry slip and several near-misses—and near-disasters—in the cars and homes of boys who belonged to poetry clubs at Lafayette or to rugby clubs at Yale.

I felt, in part, like an elder sister, or a mother even, who was giving Anya as much privacy as possible with her beau. And then, in late August, when I was beginning to shop for school and to face the fact that going to Poughkeepsie frightened me, I returned to the apartment on a Saturday afternoon after swimming at Rye with friends— I had, by then, forgiven them their youth—to find Leonard on the sofa in the living room, and Anya in a true state of fear.

His head was what I saw first, propped on a crocheted pillow that leaned against the arm rest. It was white, and I saw blue veins near the surface of the skin, and beads of perspiration that looked like oil; they didn't run or drip. He wore his polished black wingtips, and it was their position that frightened me. They didn't touch, nor did they lie as if he sprawled at rest; they were apart because his legs were slightly apart, the dark blue poplin suit soaked onto them by sweat, to show how thin his thighs and calves were. There was a terrible weakness in his posture, a sense of the exhaustion of resources. His hands lay on his stomach, barely, as if he hadn't strength enough to lift his arms. His breathing was shallow—I looked to be certain that he breathed. He opened his eyes, and their blueness made his pallor seem worse. He smiled and then his lips made the shape one makes to whistle. He was showing me that he knew how he looked, and that he felt as ill as he appeared, and that he, and disability, and us together—me poised over and before him in uselessness and perplexity—were something of a joke we each understood. But no noise came from his lips. I touched my own lips with my index finger, as if hushing him, as if dispelling the confession he would make, and I turned away quickly to find Anya in the bedroom, where I knew she would be, smoking Player's and crossing her legs.

I sat on the bed beside her. But she sat up taut, so I moved away. "It's the heat," she said.

"It looks like more than the heat, Anya."

"It's the heat *because* it's more than the heat. He has a bad heart. He's been seeing doctors."

"What are they planning to do?"

"Nothing. Medication. They say he's too old for the kind of surgery he needs."

And that, as much as Leonard's condition, was what made her start to weep. I think she had been waiting in that darkened bedroom filled with cigarette smoke and the hum of air-conditioning for someone to whom she could state that cruelty: that she, a slender woman in shorts and a halter, a woman with a young throat atop a body that was no disgrace despite the varicose veins, a woman who for years had conducted in perfect French an *affaire* with a man of gentle elegance—she, such a woman, now faced the continuation of a lesson she had received when my father left us years before. The lesson was about things running down—respect and trust and strength, and finally time.

I said, "Anya, can I ask you something?"

She sniffed and wiped her face with the back of a pale beautiful wrist. "When you ask if you can ask, Susu—Suzanne—it means you know you shouldn't ask it. Do you really need to?"

I said, "Do you and Leonard make love?"

She exploded into tears then, perhaps because her answer—not the impertinence or heartlessness of the question—was another segment of the lesson she must learn. "We used to," she said, as she tried to catch her breath.

"He can't anymore?"

"Suzanne!"

And her genuine dignity, a surprising muscularity of tone, her wonderful slight carriage, the beauty of her hair and neck, and certainly the specter of Poughkeepsie and my sense of the blackness beyond what I managed to know—all brought me into her arms, leaning over her, smelling her hair, wishing that I wept only for her.

Her letters to school described his frailty and determination. My visits home confirmed them. They were together a great deal, and Leonard came to 50th Street with gifts—a book, a pen from Mark Cross, a scarf purchased at Liberty on one of his transatlantic trips. I grew accustomed, over that first year of school and then the others, to his slower walk, a loss of tension in his bearing, his need to pause and catch his breath, the permanent pallor of his face, his need for naps. His illness aged my mother, and I accepted that as well: I felt ten years older than I was, and it seemed appropriate to me that my mother should not look young. Leonard worked harder than before, and Anya tried to convince him to retire.

I was studying in my room at home one weekend, with the door ajar, when I heard her ask him, again, to slow his pace. He snapped at her, "I have to provide for a *wife—* remember? She's getting on, like us."

That was in my sophomore or junior year, and on the New York Central to Poughkeepsie that Sunday evening I stared out the window at the Hudson, which in the last sunlight looked like ice although it was nearly May, and I thought as hard as I could about Leonard's wife. I knew that he had been married to her for some thirty years. I knew that their child was grown and away. I knew that they maintained a home in Westchester County but that Leonard, complaining of fatigue, had furnished an apartment in the east forties where he stayed during the week. I knew that he often found a reason for staying in the city over weekends as well—that is, he found an alibi to broadcast in Westchester; I knew the reason. I wondered how much his wife knew, and I fell asleep refusing to believe that she didn't know it all.

I spent a week preparing for final exams, and made use of one of Leonard's lectures. This one had been on the Dead Sea scrolls. He had lent me three books and had told me what he knew. As I studied, I heard the low sweet voice, smelled the breath of decay, saw the round-shouldered posture he more and more assumed, and the sad ironic smile—a kind of shyness, I concluded—on the handsome white face. And I studied history, and Platonic posturings—" 'But, sirs, it may be that the difficulty is not to flee from death, but from guilt. Guilt is swifter than death' "—and thought, again, that Dryden really needn't have bothered. I was studying Leonard Marcus, my mother's lover, and wondering why he, who had in spirit left his wife, was of a different category of being from my father, who had left his wife in fact. It pleases me to remember that, although I couldn't answer the question, I knew that Leonard Marcus *was* different. And thinking of my small rattled mother, or of Leonard's low devoted tones caressing the history of the Jefferson Administration, say, or of the angry assertion of his wife's need for money in old age, I am now—callow an impulse as it is—proud.

Leonard was not allowed to drink, and I had sworn myself to ignore his married life. We renounced those imperatives together in New York after he had returned from a business trip to Paris, and after I had begun my first semester at Columbia Law. Leonard called me at John Jay Hall and asked me to meet him at the Top of the Towers. I dressed nervously and too stylishly, and was quiet as we rode the elevator to the top of the Beekman Arms. We sat at a little table on the terrace and looked over the stone balustrade at the river, which, from that enormous distance, looked clean. The entire city looked clean and manageable, and knowing that it was an illusion helped me swear to myself that for this shrinking man who always, now, was out of breath, I would sustain whatever illusions he required of me. The winds up there were strong, despite the heat of late September, and I thought Leonard shivered. But when I suggested that we move indoors, he smiled that shy smile, shrugged his shoulders, and ordered drinks. He bought me a brandy

Alexander, as if I were half child and we were combining the magic of a milkshake and the necessity that a dignified law student enjoy strong drink.

I felt like someone's daughter.

Leonard held my hand, then put it down as you would place Baccarat on a marble table—with deference to its quality, with care because it was fragile. And he began—precisely as if he were telling me of the rebel zealot Jesus, or of the building of Washington, or of the regulations governing off-shore fishing in Europe—to deliver another lecture. But this one was about his life.

"My wife is named Belle. Did you know that? She's a very tall woman, nearly as tall as you are. But she has bad feet, something to do with the instep, it's terribly painful, and she tends to shuffle. For some reason, that makes her look shorter. When I tell you this, you should try to see her as someone who is short. She has friends on Long Island, younger than she—younger than I—who are very much involved in the restoration of Colonial furniture. Do you care about Colonial furniture?" He actually paused, waited to know, and I am quite certain that he did wonder, even at the moment, about my interests. I shook my head and lit another Chesterfield—he had to cup his hands around mine to shelter the flame from the wind—and then Leonard continued.

"This happened last week, before I went to Paris. Did you know I'd been there? I'll have to tell you about it. A ship seems to have disappeared, although the client insists it was sold to the Egyptians, under Panamanian registry, for purposes involving proscribed shipments to Northern Ireland. Our adversaries insist that the bill of lading was received and entered at Marseilles. The original owners are Americans—it's out of Eric Ambler, did you ever read him?" He laughed and threw his hands up, shook his head. "It's nonsense, and they're all crooks. But I want you to know about last week, before my trip. Belle was supposed to spend the weekend with her friends, and they asked if I could drive out with them. It was time to say yes, and I did, and we met at their apartment, at University Place, to go together to their house on the Island. You know how I've been—sometimes my energy is pretty poor." This time he didn't smile.

"Without going into details, let me say that I was pretty punk about it. Just as we were about to leave, I told Belle that I was too tired for the drive and that I'd go back to my apartment. She was furious, but she wasn't surprised." He looked at me so intensely that I looked away. "I want you to understand some of the complexities of our assumptions, Belle's and mine. At any rate, I did go back, and they went on to Long Island.

"My understanding is that Belle became worried about me"—he signaled for more drinks, brandy Alexander for me, white wine for him—"and woke up the poor host and made him drive her all the way back to New York at two in the morning, in a nasty rain. She has a key, of course, and let herself into my apartment."

"You weren't there," I said.

"No."

"Because you moved in with Anya after I went uptown to Columbia."

"That's not inaccurate."

"You keep the other place—"

"As a cover. In an Eric Ambler novel, it would be called that, yes." Leonard tried to smile, sipped his wine, frowned at it.

"And you sort of live part-time with Anya?"

He shrugged, raised his eyebrows, said, "It's a simple clarity for a complex situation—but, yes. Yes."

"Can I be your law clerk, Leonard?"

He grinned, with all his teeth this time, saying, "You mean you're my student? You flatter me that much?"

"Meaning I admire you very much."

He said, "You'll be *Law Review* and start someplace so prestigious—"

"Can I? Can I ask you again at the end of the year?"

He blushed, like a young man having drinks with a girl at one of the city's romantic saloons, and he said, "Yes. Please."

"Thank you, Leonard."

"But listen," he said. "She came into an empty apartment and looked around—it's tiny, a sofa bed, a kitchenette, a bathroom and closet. But she looked. And not only wasn't I there, there were barely signs that I'd *been* there. I don't know precisely what she began to know, but she began to know it. It was four in the morning by then. She sat there, by herself, not reading, not looking at television. She simply sat. Probably in the dark. And then, around six, she called the police and asked what to do. They told her she could file a missing persons report. What would that achieve? she asked. Nothing, they told her, except list me as missing and cause my name to be checked in emergency rooms and at the medical examiner's office. She thought there was no point in that, she said. She said she knew that if I were sick or dead she'd find out fairly soon. Then she went down to Grand Central and rode home. She reached me at the office later that morning. I assured her that I had been all right. I told her not to worry herself."

"And she accepted that?"

"She said she supposed foreign clients had arrived on a late plane and that I had to meet them."

"You let her believe that?"

"I didn't really answer. I told her I'd be home that weekend and told her to take care of herself, and we hung up."

"Leonard, she believed you?"

"We believe what we need to, I suppose."

"Is that true?"

He clasped his hands before him, in the air. The tips of his fingers were white and substanceless beneath the skin; they held the imprint of whatever they pressed upon. Shrugging his shoulders, he said, "It *sounds* true."

"Leonard, everything sounds true if you say it right."

"Dealing with other people's truth *can* be a self-indulgent process," he said. And then, as if to assure me that his remark was not meant merely to discipline me, he added, "We have been self-indulgent, I suppose, in a sense. Though we've been waiting for this. We're waiting now." And I didn't know which *we*—my mother and he, or someone else's mother and he—he meant.

I finished my drink, and he ordered another round, and then he finished his. We sat in silence through the arrival of the drinks, and through our consumption of them, and through the waiter's arrival with more. I smoked a lot and tried to think hard. Leonard waited patiently for me to have a reaction, or to discern what it was. I lit another cigarette—he cupped his hands for me again—and I blew smoke out, feeling that my tongue was raw, my throat sore, my head filled with childish exclamations and masterful formulations and the tune of a Robert Hall radio jingle. It was dark over the river now, but bright on the terrace, and ships were glimmering like fish as their superstructures caught the light the river absorbed. I said, "Life is confusing, Leonard," and he was decent enough to try to keep his lips from curving. But he couldn't, and then I couldn't, and we laughed—whooped, really—until he walked around to my chair, leaned from behind to kiss my cheek, and then gripped my arm to help me up and get me to a cab.

A year after his death—he died in his sleep, and in Westchester—I was spending the weekend helping my mother clean and cook for a party she'd decided it was necessary to give. As I vacuumed and put things away, grinding my teeth because I should have been uptown at my desk, I looked, thinking of my books, at the bed-side bookcase. I saw *Judgment on Deltchev* by Eric Ambler. I thought of the Beekman Towers and Leonard's lesson; I had been trying to understand it since he'd offered it to me, and particularly since his death—since the funeral we felt we couldn't attend. I think our absence would have provoked his hesitant smile, but also grave pity for Anya and, I think, actual understanding of her relief at not having to watch him buried. Anya knew of his death when she read it in the *Times*.

With the vacuum cleaner bellowing, I opened the book, saw Balkan names and descriptions of fear and subterfuge, and then a shade of baby blue—a piece of notepaper. I laughed, because only in stories and in the most arcane probate cases will a letter from the dead fall from among the pages of a book. But I was sure that I had found such a letter, and I did not laugh anymore. In the roar of Anya's Electrolux, air pouring from an unstoppered vent, the old motor getting louder as it got hotter, I sat on my mother's bed and opened the folded single sheet.

It was six-by-nine—perhaps half an inch longer each way
—and where it had been folded, yellow-brown had sup-
planted the blue. A lion was engraved in the upper left-
hand corner, and in the right it said *Hôtel Lotti, 7 et 9,
Rue de Castiglione, Paris*. And below, nothing. No message I could read, no reminder, no clue. It was simply a
bookmark, a convenience—it had nothing to say.

I smelled the motor grinding and meat cooking in the
kitchen and the harsh intimate scent of Anya's Russia
Leather. I was made physically sick by the blankness of
the paper, its neat precise folds in which the brown dis-
colorations pooled. I folded it and put it back in the
book, and I thought of Leonard in a hotel room that
smelled of paint. He lay on the long wide wooden bed
in the Hôtel Lotti. Over a chair hung his trousers, wrinkled from the airplane, and on the bathroom doorknob
hung his jacket, heavy with passport case and pens. He was
in undershorts and undershirt, and his long black hose
were held to his thin white calves by garters, black and
tight. His feet nearly touched, and one arm lay on his
chest while the other held *Judgment on Deltchev*. He
was reading of failures and fealties, the corruptions of the
sub-rosa world, and Anya was on 50th Street, and I was
studying torts, and the man who had fathered me was
living in Edgware, and I knew who my father was. I
heard the shallow breathing and saw his thin white skull
on the wide pillow, the dwindling body enclosed by the
patterned wallpaper of the Hôtel Lotti.

I was holding the paperback book when Anya came
in to find me sitting on her bed. The noise of the vacuum
cleaner broke around me like beach thunder. Her throat
was slack now, and the flesh of her upper arms soft. In

her black dressing gown she seemed pretentious and pathetic, too made up, as if she had costumed herself for solitude and, at the same time, me.

She turned her head to the side as she looked at me; it was a dog's motion of puzzlement, a gesture new for her, another sign of age in us both. She asked me, I think, what the matter was. But her voice did not carry through the sound of the machine.

That was when I whispered, into all that mechanical rage, to all her worn-out loneliness, that I'd been studying too hard and needed to rest. I thought of Leonard Marcus' wife and tried to picture her as short.

That was when Anya mimed across the machine to me the question I read on her lips.

She said: What? What?

TRAVELING

ALONE

IN DANGEROUS

PLACES

On a street in Berlin where I shouldn't have been, the man I was with tried to rape me standing up, against a wall that felt more greasy than cold. He had attracted me with his rage, then had attracted me more by showing the depths his rage might reach. I was certain that he would not make love unless I was crying, or bruised on a bed and silent, scared. The best I can say about me is that when we picked each other up, he looked beautiful, and he was very polite to the waiters when we left. I was holding his hand, and he should have known that I was making up my mind. But finally he was stupid. He did not believe in choice.

Beside a yellow BMW he said was his, on a street of closed shops, he pushed me into the wall and I made the decision I might have made before: I stuck two fingers into his nostrils as far as they would go and yanked up, weeping because it was his nose as much as for any other reason. He bled down onto my elbow before I pulled myself out and prodded my clothes and herded my body away past the fifteen people who had ultimately watched us. A very thin woman in a timelessly ugly blue suit was slapping her escort's expressionless face, over and over again, telling him in educated German of his cowardice. She stopped to smile at me, shake her head, nod her head, blow out, as if to cleanse me. She said to me in German, "What we don't know about that sickness. What we don't know!"

That was after the separation and before the divorce, when I was traveling alone in dangerous places, being cold and strong. I held myself by those small and desperate abstractions—cruelty, pride, honor, strength—and they were useful and inaccurate enough for me to believe —until his cable came. I was skiing with profound inability near Chamonix when he sent HAPPY APRIL DON'T YOU WISH WE HAD CHILDREN.

I cabled back NO.

But my stomach had jumped when I thought of replying and when I replied—and I began to suspect myself of subtle treasons.

Then his lawyer asked mine to ask me to return a few months later. And I wrote to his attorney, not mine, that I was coming home. I refused to wonder if the letter somehow was meant to be from me to him. At the Tem-

pelhof I did wonder, and I canceled my flight and arranged for a flight to Heathrow after drinking for a
major piece of the afternoon in a cellar bar with a German
salesman of tractors who had studied a year at Sheffield,
and who loved the word *arse*.

In London, I drank scotch, which I hate, with some
friends, whom I hate. I read the Manchester *Guardian*,
and saw three American plays and bought wool at a shop
in Bloomsbury. I saw the salesman of tractors, and he
clutched for my *arse*, and once I clutched back, and then
didn't. In Brown's, which I could no longer afford, on
a morning in May, I ate sausage and lambchop and
grilled tomatoes and eggs and answered a classified ad
in the *Guardian;* over the phone I rented a cottage in the
Lake District—maybe it was the wool. But I called the
porter and arranged to make a train to Barrow in Lanca-
shire, and I didn't write to my husband's lawyer to ex-
plain, and I went north to be silent for a week or two,
and to grow back into the size of skin I thought I usually
wore.

My landlady supported two children and the mortgage on
her old stone manor house by raising horses and selling the
pottery she threw in a kiln behind the cottage I would
stay in, where she left me to look at small rooms with oak
beams, a wide slate fireplace, a giant cupboard that said
1681 on the front, in carving that was deep and crude.
It held some old dinnerware, quite good, and once a week,
when the greengrocer left in his van, it would hold my
tinned foods.

That afternoon I sat in front of a coal and wood fire,
and I poked at the paperback books I had brought and
then settled for a color supplement from *The Observer* de-

voted to the memoirs of Lady Bird Johnson. I finished it without reading anything. I started it again, then left it on the old chair and changed clothes and went outside to find the pub I had seen when my landlady drove me in from the station.

It was bright outside at five o'clock, and the hills in a bowl around the house and road were purple and blue. I looked over grazing horses at sunlight on a meadow, where a man and a dog herded sheep. The man and the dog worked in silence. Every stone and hummock where they were cast a shadow; it looked like an etching, everything was so precise.

I thought about not crying and walked through the dooryard fence, then along the muddy track to the two-lane road, then walked on the road toward the pub without seeing anything except cows and some sheep in the road who ran from me. They were trying to enter their pasture and they couldn't find the hole they had crawled through, so they waggled their bottoms ahead of me, at my pace, stopping if I did, then waggling along when I walked again, and I was willing to understand nothing had run from me for a very long time.

In the lounge of the Feathers I sat at a small table, resting in the heat of the electric fire and drinking mild Hartley's beer. A tall thick man at the bar was looking at me. His nose looked like an American Indian's, and his oily black hair was combed straight back like a mane. His skin was pink, a baby's. I watched the heavy muscles in his bare forearms as he drank from his pint and smoked cigars, blowing the smoke out and moving his face away from the cloud.

So of course he brought two beers to my table, and of course he sat down without asking, and of course we started to talk. Once he learned my name, he said "Leslie" a great many times, at the beginning and end of statements, and in the middle of descriptions—of how shepherds used their crooks to rescue sheep from snowbanks on the fells during the worst of the winter; how he climbed a mountain called the Old Man with a rescue team to carry down American tourists who couldn't tramp, much less climb; how although he had once been a Communist, he now voted Tory and he wasn't sure why.

It was his arms I kept looking at, their dense hair, and the pressure of muscles at the skin.

Another man sat down with us, smiling too broadly, polite. His name was David, and he was a schoolteacher someplace, and he wanted to talk about Norman Mailer. I said I hadn't read Norman Mailer, that I didn't read novels anymore, and on a piece of paper from his notebook the man started to write the titles of American novels I should read.

I said, "While you're giving me all these names, could you tell me the name of this man who's been talking to me?"

David looked at him and said, "Why, that's Jack. Do you always talk to men who know your name without knowing theirs in return?"

I said, "Yes."

Jack rested both arms on the table—one lay on David's eager list—and said, "Jack Thorstein." He didn't smile. "You heard me say it *stine.*"

"Is that good or bad for you?" I said.

David pulled his list away and folded it once and handed it to me like a waiter presenting the bill. He smiled, nodded, pulled at his tie. "See you again, Leslie," he said. Then, still standing, he said, "Leslie, you must read some novels by your American writers, you know."

Jack leaned farther forward and said, "Ah, novels, they're the things now."

David smiled over our heads—there was the wall behind us, and a silly flowered curtain, and the sparse traffic outside—and he walked backward a step and then went toward the counter of the bar. Jack did not smile. He leaned back, lit a cigar, and watched me drink the dark brown beer.

There was a silence, and then I leaned back too, straightening my legs to push the list of writers into the pocket of my slacks. He watched me, then studied how I watched his eyes go over me.

I said, "Do you like novels, Jack?"

He said, "Are you familiar with the writings of Pushkin?"

"I've never met a mountaineer who read Pushkin," I said.

"Ah, well, I read a great deal, you know. And the other night, on the television, they had a sort of symposium. Several critics of literature and a couple of writers—they were talking about this new book on race. Perhaps you've heard of it? A great thing, this book. Very bold, very brave, and probably very unpopular. How far back can you trace your family line, Leslie?"

"What? Family line? You mean my ancestors?"

"Aye. Your family tree, you could say."

"Barely into the forest. I don't know, really."

He sucked at his cigar. "*Stein* means body of water in the Danish the Vikings spoke when they settled here. They're our colonists, Leslie. This town was once called

Thor-stein: God's water. I count my ancestors back nine hundred years. No, it isn't a Jewish name."

"I never asked if it was," I said.

He moved his arms and saw my eyes follow. He continued his thought as if he had not heard me—or as if I had tried to interrupt.

"What I loved about Pushkin was his sense of belonging to a great ancient tradition that had gone on for so long before him. You must have sensed that about him yourself?"

I made a noise in my throat. He looked at his beer, then drank it, then said, "And now that sense of tradition is lost. Among the Soviets, I wager. Certainly among us—look what's happening to the Lakes. The people who come in here and think in a month or less they're locals among our people. Cockney cab drivers from London who want to raise sheep!"

I said, "It's a beautiful country here."

"Aye, it's the place to live in."

"So why not cockneys too?"

"Quite simply, Leslie, because they don't belong here. They belong to their own life—the streets and the gutters and the muck their families dumped them into. Are you a Communist in America?"

"Nobody's a Communist in America," I said.

I drank my beer, and he took the empty glass from me. He went to the counter and called, "Fred! Fred, fill some glasses here!" The man behind the bar, slight and very blond, middle-aged and drunk-looking, stood at a beer pull, shoulders slumped, a cigarette in his mouth. The three other men at the bar, David among them, moved back as Jack called.

I thought of Berlin and of other places, mostly of hotels.

The bartender walked to the far end of the counter, away from Jack, and leaned onto it, holding a half pint of lager, pouring lime juice as if he hated it into the bright yellow beer. He talked to the man he was serving, and then he bent toward something under the bar.

Jack said, "Fred, now fill these glasses or we'll send you to Northern Ireland for a rest." His voice sounded as if he meant to joke.

The bartender slammed a bottle of lime syrup to the counter. He turned toward Jack and pointed a finger at him, pulled the cigarette from his mouth and threw it onto the floor. He said, "Don't you—" and then he walked toward Jack. He said, "Don't you say that fookin' word to me." The bartender took the two pint glasses from Jack and walked away toward the beer pull. He turned again and pointed, said, "Don't you say that fookin' word to me again. Son of a bitch!" He filled the glasses and banged them, slopping beer over, down in front of Jack. He put a foot up on something behind the bar and said—droned it, very low—"Don't you ever say that fookin' word to me again in your life."

Jack's head was tilted back a little, and he put both glasses on the palm of his left hand. He pulled his cigar from his mouth and blew out smoke, moving his head away from it. He watched.

The bartender leaned in toward him and whispered, "Let's you and me have a ten-minutes session in the car park, would you?"

Jack looked at him and then came back to me with the beer in one hand.

He sat, and slid my glass over, and sucked on his cigar. He said, "Fred's been upset now."

The bartender looked at us, a new cigarette in his mouth. He called, "Let's have that conversation now, Jack, you son of a fookin' bitch."

Jack moved his forearms onto the table and said, "He's an Irishman, you know."

"He's not serious, is he?"

"Oh, aye, he gets upset, you see, about the situation over there. I've been to Belfast many times for Vickers where I work. I've walked on the streets and never seen a Catholic being bothered. I wonder if it isn't the news people—their carrying on, Leslie. Exaggerating it all, you see."

"You mean he wants to *fight* you about it?"

Jack made a fist with his huge clean hand and held it up as if it were a watch he had taken from his pocket. He said, "Old Fred wouldn't do very well out there."

I looked at Jack's fist.

He said, "We get wild up here, sometimes."

"It feels like it."

"Does it, Leslie? Do you like it here?"

I said, "I'm on my way home."

"Aye, home's the place."

"For what?"

He stretched himself in his chair—I watched the knitted shirt swell out—and he said around the cigar, "It always depends, Leslie, on the home and the people going to it."

I said, "I meant America."

"Aye, there's homes and then homes in between."

"You mean where I'm living now. Tonight."

"Well, I don't know, Leslie."

"No. Sure you don't."

He didn't listen then. He leaned forward, into his language: "So you don't agree with the Communists, then? I used to. I had a card. Now I'm a foreman for Vickers, making submarines to blow up Communists with."

"You sound very pleased," I said.

"You see, Leslie, I was very deep in the local party. Very, very deep in the center of those things. And one day I looked around me"—I waited for an expression on his face to match the story, but he was listening too hard to himself—"and I saw that everywhere around me were the Jewish people. Everyone. So I had to resign."

He looked at me, but he was not bothered by what he saw. I felt as if I'd gone pale. "They were intent on using the movement for their own ends." He moved the cigar sideways in the air. "I shouldn't have been surprised. I'm not surprised now that I've done a great deal of reading about it. Their own writings say it. I've read on that subject a great deal. They were chosen to be the master race and succeed at the expense of all the other peoples of the world. That's what they believe."

"You think so?" I said.

He plowed my words away with his nose and chopping hand. "I daresay I've read plenty of books on the subject." I put my hands in my lap. "They believe, and it's their right to believe it, that they were chosen to be the master race. To use everyone else to their own ends. It's a matter of scientific record. After the ice receded, eleven thousand years ago—this is modern history we're talking about, Leslie—the agricultural peoples spread out, moving north from the Mediterranean. Modern times, Leslie. Eleven thousand years ago, after the ice receded, the agricultural people, you see, spread out, moving up from the Mediterranean. Now you'll agree that the strongest instinct in all animals, and that's men included, is to propagate their kind and populate the earth."

"Jack, no one believes that anymore. The strongest urge is mating, maybe. But that's not taking over the earth."

"And the Jewish people have always wanted to breed into places they weren't born to. That was their intention and need. Right or wrong, and I say wrong, they were following the laws of nature and their own beliefs, Leslie. I'll give them that. But I wasn't about to watch—"

I said, "*Jack!*" The men at the bar looked toward us, and the bartender gestured at us, and Dave nodded. I put my fingertips against my lips, then held my own hand. I said, "This is—the Nazis said this, Jack. They killed six million *people* for this."

"Ah," he said. His face was tranquil as he listened to himself. "I've always doubted that statistic. The people who won the Six-Day War in 1967 wouldn't have let themselves be killed like that. No, I'm certain it was far fewer than that."

I heard the bartender grunt and whisper, and then looked to see him go into the doorway of the public bar and out of sight. Jack had heard his voice, I suppose, because he put his cigar into his mouth and his glass back down on the table. He stood and looked at me—I don't know what he saw—and said, "Wait here a minute, won't you?" Then he walked past the men at the bar without speaking and then he walked out the door.

I stood too.

Dave came over, pulling at his tie. His long serious face was red. He rubbed his hand against his side. He said, "I can give you a ride to your home—the cottage. Perhaps you'd better take a lift?"

I said, "And what will he do when he decides to find me and you're there?"

"Beg your pardon? Oh. Oh, I'm married."

"Yes. Yes. But I'll walk, thank you, Dave."

I did, in my wooden clogs and fine woolen slacks. I walked from the Feathers along the two-lane road grown darker, but still with a blue brightness on it from the sun that had fallen while Jack was telling me how many fewer Jews had been killed. There were stone fences on both sides of the road, and they were as high as my head. The lichen on them seemed sometimes to glow. I heard water rushing, and the sheep bleating as I went by their grazing, and the gears of cars changing down for the hills. And I heard a car moan in low gear along the road behind me, around an S-curve between the high stone walls, pebbles popping from under the wheels. I thought of things fried and bursting—and then I heard, "Leslie?"

He said, "I'm taking old Fred home. He's hurt himself by mistake. Perhaps you'd like to join me in the front, as Fred's lying down in the back now. We could drive him to his house together, Leslie."

I stood on the wet grass near the high old fence and looked away from him, in the window, his arm protruding down along the metal of the door.

He said, "Come on now, girl. We'll have an errand of mercy and then we'll have a drink."

I said, "Please go away, Jack. I'm sorry. Please."

The engine stopped and his hand reached out. He pinched two fingers into the wool of the sweater I wore. He said, "Leslie, wouldn't you like us to have a ride?"

I stood there.

He said, "You're not afraid of me, now."

"No. I'm not. No."

"No, of course not. No one needs to be afraid of Jack."

"Don't try to scare me, Jack," I said.

"Aye, I know I can't. So then? Leslie, you're a grand woman, do you know that?"

His door lock clicked. I moved back, toward the fence. He got out and walked past me, without looking at me, and went to the other side of the car and opened the door. He stood with the door open, waiting, his car on the wrong side of the road, pressing me into the wall.

I went past him and sat down inside. The car smelled of liquor, and I twisted in the seat to look at Fred: He lay in the back, his ankles crossed, his glasses in one small hand, the other hanging to the floormat. His eyes were open and wet with tears. They looked toward the roof. When Jack sat down, the car swayed.

"He's fine, Leslie. He got himself into trouble is all. But he's grand, really. Aren't you, Fred?"

I watched the bartender look up, at nothing. Then I turned around to look out the windshield as we drove around sharp curves.

"He lives in a shabby council house—it isn't more than ten or twelve years old, I believe. He's one of those new sorts of people I believe I told you about."

"New sorts of people?"

"Aye. But we needn't talk about them."

"Did you hurt him?"

"I believe I did, Leslie."

"Shouldn't we take him to a doctor, then?"

"I hurt him in his pride most of all. It's what kills a person. You can understand that."

I looked at him, but he was watching the road.

Where the road widened at a T-junction, there were three two-family houses back behind stone fences. Jack stopped in front of them, and when he pulled the handbrake on, Fred came into the driving mirror, staring for my eyes. His breath came over with its whiskey and vomit as he sighed. He was out of the car then, and Jack walked behind him toward one of the houses.

I heard Fred's high, sad voice say, "I don't want you in my house, Thorstein!"

A door opened, a woman stood against light, and Fred said, "I'll see you banned from the bar, Thorstein."

Then the men fell into the light, it was dimmed, and then it was gone.

When Jack got back in, I smelled his soap and sweat. I looked ahead as though we were moving, and I said, "I would like you to drive me to the cottage I'm staying in. I can't imagine what to say to you anymore, and I don't feel witty enough to try. Let's get the girl home, Jack."

He started the car and went into a tight turn, then straightened out and drove quickly. After a while he turned the parking lights on, but the deep blue of the air made them useless. I smelled something foreign and I sniffed, and then he looked at me, leaned his face toward the floor, grunted, knocked the handbrake off. The car seemed to rise an inch and go faster.

I said, "Is this how I go home?"

He said, "I felt sorry for Fred."

"I'm sure he appreciated your concern. And his wife."

"Aye, it was all unnecessary."

I watched Jack's hands as they steered, and his arms, and I looked at the fences wobbling beside us.

He laughed. He said, "I want you to walk on the common with me, Leslie. You'll see what I'm made of, this land we have here."

"I've been on the common."

"No you haven't, girl."

"I don't *want* this," I said.

"Leslie, you're safe."

That's when I didn't think so. The road grew narrower, and I saw water on the left, part of a rocky beach, then cliffs on both sides of us, and then it opened out to bare spots of rock and earth going up to hills. The mountains were above them, over us then, and in the light that was left I saw bright yellow flowers and furry sheep.

Maybe I asked. He said, "Gorse."

"Thank you."

He drove the car up near a cliff of gray rock, wrinkled like very old skin. He took the keys from the ignition and walked around to open my door. I looked down. I saw the ground covered with a kind of dark red straw. He said, "Bracken."

"Oh," I said, "I don't care."

"Yes you do, Leslie. Come with me. Here." He held my arm near the shoulder and his fingers lay against the side of my breast before he closed his hand. "Come with me."

He pulled me out and I went, up along a sort of path where the sheep ran away from us, climbing, and lambs called until a deeper bleat answered, and then the calls ticked on and off until the ewes and lambs called together at the same spot and then went still. The wind blew harder where we were, and he stayed below me, still holding on, but pushing upward now. I went as fast as I could to ease the force of his hand. At a level place where

I tried to stand and catch my breath he paused beside me, then pushed again. I stepped into thick wet moss, then softer stuff, and my feet were wet to the ankles. I stopped, then stepped aside, pulled away from his hand, but he held on. I said, "Really, I don't care."

He let go. I was pulling, and I fell when his hand released me. I turned sideways, then over, and crawled on my hands and knees, then stood, one clog missing in the bog someplace. He stood with his arms across his chest and said, "Leslie, it's a different world here."

I sat down and pulled my knees to my chest, put my arms around them, held my hand to keep the shape intact.

He said, "Aye. Where everything that happens is cruel." He sat down where he was and pulled his knees against his chest, held them with the circle of his arms. They were white in the darkness, and I watched them.

He said, "This land we're on, that's what I wanted you to see. I followed you for that. Aye. Here. I live in this" —his hands made arcs, and he leaned a little backward as he showed me the darkness and the hills that floated on it—"this is what I am."

"All right," I said.

"I think that's what the people are after, Leslie. This. What you look for."

He kept his hands wide, and I saw that he wasn't waving at the mountains anymore. His arms funneled all the dark blue air down into himself. "No," he said. "You're a person in need, I think. Do you not know yourself?"

I fell forward until I stood. Then I kicked in the moss and ferns and high grass until I found the other clog. I watched for him to move, but he didn't, and I put the clog on and walked down a little, my feet sideways to the slope so I wouldn't slip. Then he did move, and I stopped moving and held my face where it was, looking down and away.

He said, "You need strength placed into your life, Leslie. You know it." He moved again, and I waited for him to come down to me, but he stayed where he was.

I did too, remembering how, on a street in New York where I should not have lived, in a flat we couldn't afford, my husband stalked me in our four rooms, bristling, huffing, sighing into magazines, turning the TV on and off, drinking water loudly in the kitchen, waiting for me to hear him sigh or swallow or sit or stand or pace the chocolate carpet from the bonsai tree to the Workbench sofa to the architect's lamp, rubbing at his throat and temples, posing for the film the world was making of our lives.

THE LAND OF
THE FREE

Billy slipped off the scaffolding three times that day, nothing serious, but pretty meaningful to him since he was a hundred feet up and stupid enough to think we'd let him die for his sins. In his red wool hunting jacket, he looked like a flag on a map. That's how flat the land looked from where I was working, above him toward the silo's top. I let him dangle a while, the wind whipping him in little circles, and then I called down, "You tie that bowline tight, Billy?"

He laughed because he thought we wanted him to be brave. But when we pulled him up and held him onto the scaffold, he was white and maybe a year older. He giggled like a kid. It was cold. The wind never stops up there, and I could see snow in the raggedy rows of Stanley Everett's field gleaming like ice. Everything was white and brown except for Stanley's tractors and the old red barn, the falling red wooden silo beside us. We were up on the new bright blue aluminum silo ready to get the roof done, and I was glad to be close to finished because of the cold and because we could get the flag part of it done with and Billy home. He always asked to put the stars and stripes sticker onto the side, below the top, and I always let him. It didn't matter a damn to the rest of us and it struck me as waste motion—a hundred-foot blue silo with a six-foot Old Glory up there. It was as wasted as playing the anthem before a football game. A little less flag and a little more money into the economy was my way of thinking about it. Stop waving and start governing, I say. But Billy liked to crawl around with his hands half-iced, slapping up the sticker the way someone on every other crew on every other silo slaps it up. All right, I used to think, put your flag up and then go home and grouse at your wife and bitch at your kids and play with your TV knobs. I used to say to myself, All right, this is his last day. I never fired him, though, bad as he was at his work. It got to where we needed someone stupid to remind us not to fall off the job and die in some farmer's yard covered with icy shit and chickens.

So Billy was sitting on the scaffold, chattering and making jokes, and the rest of us were checking the safety lines and getting ready to hoist the roofing frames up when Sam Harvey's daughter, the big one who's a nurse in Morrisville, came in her little car to call me down. I went with her when she asked me to, when she started telling me what she and her parents had seen two afternoons before, across the road at Buddy Preston's house. I called up, "Billy, don't you slip again, hear? You used up your luck."

He waved. He was too stupid to think I was serious. And I went along with Cornelia Harvey to the hospital because Buddy Preston had sent in need. It wouldn't have done not to go.

My legs were jammed up in the little car and it was a long drive. They'd taken Buddy to the hospital where Cornelia worked as soon as they'd done the first aid, because his wife thought he should be where there were neighbors and friends. They had to take him thirty miles to get to a neighbor or friend. No one who *was* his neighbor really wanted the job, and Buddy didn't have a friend, except maybe his new landlady in Smyrna, because he said he liked her sour cream cake. So they agreed with Serena, who is his wife, when she decided Buddy had to be in Morrisville where Cornelia, who had known him all her life and liked him hardly a day of it, could see to Buddy's bedpan and meals.

There wasn't much to look at, so I looked at Cornelia for a while. She was chubby but without any tits on her and, anyway, bundled as she was in her coat, I couldn't have seen what she had if there *was* much of anything to see. Her legs were like poles, fat and round and straight down from her knees to her ankles. She had a flat nose and thin lips and a lot of dandruff on her glasses and collar. She'd wanted to get away from home and the farthest she could go was Morrisville. And then she'd come home for a visit, probably just to try herself out with the family again, and there they'd been, tired of each other and looking out the dooryard window, waiting for something to come along that they could talk about, and that's when they saw Buddy on the porch, and his kid, and Serena coming home from the hospital with Buddy's daughter, who was better-looking than Cornelia but not worth half a mouthful of Cornelia's spit.

We'd known about the accident Serena got into, and most of us had dropped some money into the coffee can in the P.O. for flowers. She never got to sniff them even. Because there she was, her broken collarbone set and casted, resting in her semiprivate, all set to stay because they thought maybe her concussion was bad, when Buddy came in, just eyes and mouth. You always saw Buddy's eyes first—half-squinted and looking as if they never closed in sleep, blown up goggled like a bug's by his thick glasses, and crazy as hell. And then, if he did talk, it was like hearing somebody who was dead brought back for just a minute to describe what the corpse worms feel like. You were always sorry when Buddy did decide to speak. Seeing him was bad enough—thick, short, pale, and looking like a full-time victim who had grown damned used to it.

We heard once how his son—he was eleven, and he had his father's eyes—had forgotten to do a chore because he was building one of those plastic ship models. That was when Buddy lived at home full-time instead of only weekends. Buddy saw the shed wasn't cleared, or the trash bags weren't loaded into his truck, and he went upstairs to the boy Peter's room, not talking, and reached out and crushed the model in his hands while the boy watched. And still not talking, not looking at his son, Buddy walked on out.

The boy played best with littler kids. But he got

rough and hurt them. He couldn't play with the ones his age. They got like dogs and smelled his fright and wanting, and they beat him up.

And that's who was waiting on the side porch, Peter and his father, when Cornelia and her parents looked out their dooryard window. Buddy had been off shift for a while, Cornelia figured, watching TV with his landlady in Smyrna, when his wife, whom he had left a month ago and whom he didn't give any money to, had been driving home from her work as a waitress. Somebody turned their car in front of a tractor-trailer rig that jackknifed on 12B, and the trailer, an empty, had spun Serena's old car off the highway and into a post the electric company had put into the ground but hadn't hooked up yet. The fire company took her to the hospital and somebody came to the restaurant where Buddy's daughter worked and which her mother had just gone home from. The girl not only carried coffee and skinny pizza, but she set up appointments with gentlemen and kept them in the back seats of their cars. For appointments in trucks, so the joke went, she charged cold-weather bonuses and metal-bed tax.

So the daughter called the father, and he was concerned. He didn't send them money, and he'd helped produce two kids not fit for more than a municipal zoo or a casualty ward, and he'd put their house up for sale and moved out to a rented room a dozen miles away, and he came home on weekends with his eyes to hang around and not talk and get his laundry done and hot meals. But he was concerned.

They found out how concerned, Cornelia said, when the daughter and wife heard him all the way from the emergency room, complaining that if Serena was all right then she had better not be kept there just so the hospital could take his money for a night's stay.

Cornelia said he said, "You running a hospital or a hotel?" She heard this from the daughter and it sounds right.

The nurse there said, "You know it's a hospital, and you know enough about it to keep your voice down."

"Oh well," Buddy said, "I thought maybe it was all right to talk this loud because in hotels they let you talk the way you want, being as how they want your business. Ain't that what you're giving us here? The business? When I need a hotel, sister, why I guess I can find one with cabins for a little privacy and maybe rates a whole hell of a lot cheaper. So why don't you check her out right now, hey? And don't bother with a bellhop, she can carry the bags by herself."

Then Buddy left, because he'd given his instructions. And the next day, he was standing on his side porch for Cornelia and her family to watch, while his son who already had his legacy, those eyes, and who didn't need to expect any more from his family and who wouldn't get any more if he did, was throwing a calf rope over the lowest limb of their side-yard maple, doing it again and again, because he didn't know how to play with toys, Cornelia's mother said. Her father wondered where the boy stole the rope from. Buddy was standing there, looking across Stanley Everett's road-front field down to the iron bridge where the road starts up for hills and Stanley's farmyard. Peter was throwing his rope and pulling it down and throwing it.

Then the daughter's car came in, real slow, and Buddy stood up straight, then pushed his shoulder against the porch post and slouched at it. He began to clean his pockets out as the car came up the drive. First he did his side pockets, one at a time, folding them out, picking at lint caught in the lining, shoving the pocket back in, each one in turn. He went to the upper pockets and was doing them when Peter left the calf rope hanging onto the limb and walked over to the porch to stand below it, near his father, while his sister went around to help their mother back herself out of the car and walk slowly in. Buddy didn't look at the woman—he kept picking his pockets inside out. Peter watched them both.

We were coming down the Morrisville hill, past the State Police barracks, which was a little white house with an aluminum door on the front that had the initial S for State built into the middle, then past the agricultural college, and then we came into the parking lot at the hospital. Cornelia turned the motor off but sat where she was. "Me and my folks just watched," she said. "It was all we had to do. You know what they're like. All they are's the same. You can't stay there for long, you know?" She said, "I can't figure out why I go there anymore."

I was trying to move my knees to where they'd be comfortable, but in a little car like that, you're not supposed to be comfortable. You're supposed to feel cribbed so you think you're saving money. All I was saving was circulation. That's real economy.

Cornelia said Serena went past Buddy without looking anyplace except the stairs and the floor of the porch. The daughter opened the door and helped her in, and Peter watched them go, then he went too. Buddy picked at his pockets and looked down Stanley Everett's field.

After a while of Buddy's standing like that, the daughter came out and talked to him and he nodded. He folded his pocket back and went inside. "We kept watching," Cornelia said. "We might as well have. There would not have been much to say if we'd turned our faces back in. You know."

It didn't take long for Buddy to come back out, though. He walked slow, off the porch and around the side and back to the shed, out of sight. They waited. Nobody came after him. They waited some more. Then he came back around, with his double-edged felling ax. He didn't look at the house, Cornelia said, but went along the drive to the side-yard tree, the big maple Peter had left his rope on. He started in to cutting at it. He was sloppy, he always was—his house showed it and his children showed it. His life was long evidence against him. But he was strong, for all his sickly face and thick glasses and his lips that always looked purple, and even though the chips blew where they shouldn't have, he was making quite a dent.

Peter came out then, and stood off to the side to watch. Buddy rested sometimes, but not for long, and never looking at his son. Then he went back to hacking at the tree the way a hungry kid chops at meat. But Buddy got into that tree. He was working at it when the sun was going down, near half past four, and he even figured, in the darkness and for all his fatigue, how to make the tree fall away from the electric wires and across his gravel drive. Cornelia said, "It sounded like a bomb went off. Peter jumped when it hit. So did we. It gave us something to talk about. That was a piece of luck."

Buddy couldn't stop with that. Of course, I don't know why he started, so I don't know why he went on, and Cornelia didn't, and according to her, her parents never could know anything, much less this. In the darkness like that, tired and more crazy than he usually was, he started in to lop the little branches and chop at the big ones. That's when the ax slid sideways along the small branch he was raking at, taking it easy. It skittered into his calf, right below the knee, and sank there like the bone and gristle were sausage, and it stayed in where it was.

Cornelia said Peter screamed like a pig whose throat's cut too slow. Everyone came, including Serena, who was already crying and wailing when she hit the storm door at the porch. And they stopped the bleeding quick because Cornelia came fast—"Let me tell you, I needed something to do by then," she said—and they drove him to Morrisville because Serena thought his friends and neighbors should be with him when Buddy was in need.

She finally let us get out of that goddamned small car and walk across the parking lot and through the emergency room, where a kid was crying with a broken wrist, and up in the elevator to where Buddy had a private room. Serena said he ought to be by himself, Cornelia told me. "I thought she was right," Cornelia said. "He could infect a *stone*."

Serena was there, white and sick, her arm bound up and her face a scramble—it looked like she didn't know whether to scream or laugh or ask me for money. She thanked me for coming and I said of course. Peter sat next to his father's bed and his father didn't look at him. Peter smiled, like he was showing off a new dog. He looked proud. I couldn't do more for him than nod.

The daughter wasn't there, and maybe that's why Cornelia snorted when she left, saying, "I'll be outside."

Serena whispered, "Wouldn't you like to stay, Corny?"

"No, I really wouldn't," Cornelia said.

That left me. I said, "Hello, Buddy. How's the foot?"

"They didn't take it off," he said. It was like gravel spattered onto pinewood, the noise he made.

"Of course they didn't," I said.

He said, "That's right, all right, but not because they didn't want to. They just couldn't find someone who'd buy it off 'em at a profit yet. I'm waiting to hear they got a buyer any day."

"Well, I guess you are," I said. I wanted to take a leak or spit. I didn't know which I wanted more. And then I wanted to get back and drive past the silo and get back home and stay there a while. Get drunk and laugh and just stay in.

"What's that you wanted to ask me, Buddy? Cornelia said there was—"

"This ain't a professional call," he said. "I don't need no silos built nor barns repaired, understand?"

Gravel on pinewood coffins, I decided. His face was yellow on the pillow and his lips looked like he'd been biting at them. Serena ducked her head and looked past her sling at the floor. Peter smiled and showed me his big teeth under bright red gums.

I tried to sound easy when I said, "No charge, Buddy, I'm glad to come and help. How can I help?"

He said *Whoof!* or something like that, and I guess his leg hurt deep and very bad. His face went yellower and then came back to the color it had been, and that was awful enough.

Stones bouncing onto wood again when he said, "I want you to tell me—those big damn flags you put up."

"On the silos? Up at the top?"

"They're the ones. Now, I want to know this, understand me?"

"What about them?"

He said, "I want you to tell me. When you get all done—"

"Almost done."

"All *right*! Almost done. All right. When you do it, when you put them there. There must be one every half a mile in every direction in the whole stunk-out county, don't you think? Every place you look, there's wood silos rotting down and those big shiny blue ones next to 'em with their flags. Now, I'm asking you—does the farmer have a say, or do you slap the goddamned flags up there whether he asks you to or not?"

Peter smiled and shrugged his shoulders and smiled wider.

Serena looked at the floor and shook her head.

"I'm asking you," Buddy said, "if the farmers get to choose. You hear me? Do you give 'em a choice is what I want to know."

I said, "Aw, hell, Buddy," and I made believe to smile and then I answered him.

I lied.

F A M I L Y

C I R C L E

Ian's grandfather summoned him with sneezes. Bright silver light from the leaded windows behind his grandfather
made the dust a steady snow, falling from nowhere onto
the old man's shoulders and the polished wood desk. Large
in the morning light, he sat under an avalanche of shiny
fineness, always being buried where he sat—slow storms
of dust fell over him into his shadow on the smooth
golden oak, disappearing—always untouched. From the
doorway the old man was magical, and Ian watched
as his grandfather crossed his arms and held himself by
the shoulders and squeezed at the brown tweed cloth he

wore and hunched his shoulders and pushed his chin down onto his chest and shuddered and closed his eyes and shook out the sneeze with an open-mouthed roar. He wiped the coarse sleeve across his mouth and nose—the left arm now hugged his heart—and like a cat licking fur, he rubbed the same sleeve on the desk, slowly back and forth, cleaning. When he saw Ian in the doorway, a little higher than the sculpted metal knob, the old man said, "What? *What?*" and Ian blew away.

Ian's mother was changing Stuart's diaper—here they called it nappy, but his mother said it smelled the same in England as it did in America—and Ian stood in his room and looked around the corner of the high cupboard that, with a dark green curtain, divided where he slept from the smaller room where his mother and Stuart had a double bed and a crib. He watched as she rolled Stuart over and swabbed him with a wash rag, then turned him over again to poke him in the stomach.

Ian held himself and watched. Then he stopped smiling and backed away in his high black Wellingtons and his tight American jeans and went down the wooden steps into the main room, where they had their little kitchen and their dining table and couch and the fire that smoked. There were wooden beams on the low white ceiling, and dark chunks of wood floated in the white plaster walls. Ian stood in the room and they laughed upstairs. He took an apple down from the little refrigerator top and the sharp knife from the table. He sliced the apple, then took bread from the cupboard and made two sandwiches— chunks of thick-skinned apple between slices of bread. He put them on the wide white plates and carried them up the steps. At the doorway to his room he called, "It's okay,

Mom, I got breakfast for us. The baby can wait for his. I got us our breakfast first because we're bigger."

Brenda was in the field with the six horses, spreading hay from two bales in a wheelbarrow that she had slid, squeaking, from the old stables next door to the stone coalhouse and the little stone cottage where Ian and his mother and Stuart were staying. Next to their cottage was the big house, with its chimneys at either end. The grandfather stood in front of his house, looking down the walk and over the yew hedge and the stone fence to where Brenda, small and skinny in her dark green duffel coat and jeans and Wellingtons, fed the horses in the rain. He saw what the boy saw—a pony trying to enter the white and black mare.

Ian, in his yellow slicker and hat, sitting under the overturned canvas-and-tubing sun chaise, called, "He's putting a baby into her, Grampa. We'll have puppies soon, won't we?" The mare kicked away at the pony.

High in his dark tweed sportcoat, rocking on his shoes with their built-up commando soles, the grandfather looked at the boy, and ran his big hand over his pink scalp and the black and white strands that crossed over it. "Puppies," he said. "Ian, when horses have babies, they're called *foals*. Foals, lad. Can you say that?"

Ian said, "Foals."

His grandfather watched Brenda stand in the circle of mud and manure while the horses and ponies ate at the six stations of hay she'd made. At some signal no one ever saw, one horse would think of changing his station and another would respond, moving from his so that the first one could move, and then they all would move, in a slow rainy dance, while Brenda stood there in the center.

"Brenda's good," the grandfather said.

Ian's mother came up from the cottage, carrying Stuart, both of them covered by the white canvas raincoat she held like a tent. She said, "Brenda's got a crooked nose."

His grandfather said, "Got it the good way—she was twice kicked, had it broken twice, never set, never in hospital for it. She's as tough as you. She's tougher."

"She's twenty-five years old, Daddy."

"Aye, all of that. She qualifies, all right."

His mother said, "For *what*?"

His grandfather hugged his chest and ducked his face and wrenched his mouth about and let the sneeze curl out of his mouth and nose. He wiped his face with his sleeve.

Stuart said, "Toooo!"

His mother said, "Punishment."

His grandfather said, "Dinner," and went inside.

Brenda was wearing a black halter and her dungarees and boots, and a scarf held her long brown hair in place behind her, on the neck. She rode out with three pony-trekkers shifting and wobbling like potato sacks on their thin saddles. She led them across the two-lane road and up a small access road that went to the foot of the fells. She waved to Ian. She had dropped the butt of her filtered cigarette on the dust and stones inside the green metal gate Ian closed for her, then stood on, climbing the rungs, waving back.

When Ian jumped off the gate, the morning sun was high and hot. Sheep across the road moaned, and a truck coming down the 1:7 hill from the quarry at Broughton Moor filled the fields with the sound of its straining. The boy turned and saw that the small herd of two-year-old cattle in the outer field had followed him, were standing in a semicircle behind him, heads lowered, watching. As he moved, a white and gray heifer jumped backward and threw its face up.

"Hello," the boy said. "Hello." Ian held a handful of weed up to them, and said, "Hello."

All their eyes watched.

Ian's mother lay on the sun chaise in a bathing suit that was held together at the stomach by a metal ring. Her eyes were closed and her face was covered with tiny drops of oiled sweat. Her toes danced to the music from Brenda's big brown radio which sat atop a stone wall, all that was left of a shed outside the old stables. Brenda rubbed oil onto tack, and Ian's mother lay with almost a smile on her face, moving her feet. Stuart sat on the cobbles near Brenda, holding a red and white ball against his face, watching Brenda's hands move. Ian, in Wellingtons and shorts, made a tiny house of stones and twigs. Everyone was quiet, and the radio played, and then the green metal gate two pastures down squeaked above the music and Brenda, without looking, said, "Oh, it must be another gifted horseman. I suppose I shall have to book the lot of rubbish for a ride."

Ian stood up to watch, then ran down to the gravel where cars were parked below the big house. He shouted, "Mommy, it's the police. It's the police, Mommy!"

Brenda went down to him, lighting a cigarette, then standing with it sticking out of her mouth, her lips curled hard to hold it. "It's a taxi, Ian." She called back to his mother, "Has our Ian not seen taxis before?"

The driver let the man out at the second gate, the wooden one close by the stream that Brenda had told him was a dike and that his grandfather called a beck. But Ian's mother had said he could call it a stream because that's what they had in America.

The heavy man walked up, carrying a brown leather bag with two straps, rolling a little sideways when he walked.

Brenda said, "Ian, is that what your dad looks like?"

They walked up the access road, following the rich brown mounds of horse droppings, going along the stone fences, and then through the rocky fields where there were no fences and the road took them high enough to look down steep grazing grounds with teeth of gray rock coming through the grass, and then, on their left, the hills going higher, green and gray, and then the moors beginning, ferny and darker with moss, wet, and beyond them the blueness of mountains, grainy and clear in the bright late afternoon. His father held his hand and he stopped them near a tiny fall of water which came over rocks into a small pool that drained beneath the road and ran on the other side down to the sheep below. His father said, "Are you tired?"

Ian said, "I came up here plenty of times."

His father nodded. He pulled a thick-bladed weed up, peeled it back, wetted it, put the end in his mouth, and blew. Nothing came out. He said, "It used to make a whistle when I was a kid."

Ian said, "It's probably a different kind of plant in America."

"Everything's different here, huh?"

"And they call them different things. They don't say boots, they say Wellingtons. Grampa got me these in

Ulverston. We go shopping there. Will you get boots, Daddy?"

"You think I should?"

"If you stay here, yes. Do you have enough money?"

"Yes, love, thank you."

"Because Grampa gave me some English money if you need it."

"Thank you, love."

"If you want to stay here and go for a hike or something."

"Hey, I missed you a lot, Ian."

"They have all these swamps here. Brenda calls them boggy."

"Ian, I was really missing you. And Stu, and Mommy."

Ian walked ahead of his father, past the waterfall. The boy said, "Come on, Daddy. Only next time you have to wear boots. Wellingtons. All right?"

The grandfather sat at the desk, writing with a black fountain pen on long white paper. The dust fell onto him and disappeared into his shadow, into the words that he wrote. Ian stood at the door, his hand on the knob, watching. The grandfather didn't look up. He said, "Come here."

Inside, where the books stood in all their shelves and the newspapers were curled on the table near the wide red-cushioned chair, Ian stood beside the desk and watched the dark hairs on his grandfather's hands as they moved in the shadows. He said, "Hi."

"Can you read what I'm writing?"

"I'm not old enough to read that kind. The letters are too scribbly."

"I'm writing a book. What do you think of that?"

"Is it a good book?"

His grandfather looked over the heavy tweed on his arm at Ian's face. He said, "Is that a good question?"

Ian looked up at him. He said, "That's all I could think of."

His grandfather stood up from his chair. Ian moved back. His grandfather waved his hand inside his sport-coat pocket and took out a puddle of coins. He held the palm up to his face, poked through it, pinched a big copper two-pence piece, and held it out for Ian to take. He said, "Damned good question. It's all I could think of too." He sat down, pushed himself closer to the desk, looked at the page, and then at the papers beside it. He said, "Say thank you and disappear."

"Thank you, Grampa. Should I say disappear?"

The grandfather hugged himself and ducked his head and shook, and the sneeze belched out. He panted, then rubbed his arm over the page, making some of the words run. He wiped his mouth and hugged his chest for the next one.

At dinner in the big house, they could hear Stuart crying in his room in the cottage. The grandfather brought the pork roast in from the kitchen. He said, "Anna, do you want to see to Stuart?"

Ian's mother said, "No, dear. You ask me that nearly every night, and I tell you that he's all right. That's how he goes to sleep."

The grandfather said, "Do you remember that ruckus, Harry?"

Ian's father said, "It hasn't been that long."

Brenda smoked a cigarette and said, "Did you pick the wine?"

The grandfather said, "Absolutely. And with care."

"It's too dry."

Carving, his grandfather looked up, raised his gray eyebrows, smiled. He said, "You've got the taste of a Yorkshire pig-farmer."

Brenda said, "I'm the daughter of a Yorkshire pig-farmer."

Ian said, "Brenda says she saw a pig eat a chicken once."

"A pig will take a chunk from a fair-sized man," Brenda said.

The grandfather passed a plate to Ian's father. He said, "Let's see a man take a bit of a pig, then, Harry."

Ian's mother said, "You have such elegance, Daddy."

"Yes I do, don't I? Sort of careless elegance. It's what the landed gentry are supposed to show. But I wish I had a little more land and a little less gentry."

Ian's father said, "Should I cut your meat, Ian?"

Ian said, "Yes, please."

Ian's mother said, "I'll do it. Pass me your plate."

"Can Daddy do it?"

His father put his hands in his trouser pockets and sat lower in his chair.

Brenda said, "I wonder if anyone would like a cigarette?"

Ian passed his plate. His grandfather bowed low, sat up straighter, crossed his chest with arms, and sneezed onto the roast.

Ian's mother said, "I think you've *got* a little less gentry, Daddy. God. I won't want second helpings, thank you."

Brenda held the cigarette with her lips and said, "I think the old boy's allergic to horses."

In the stone barn, half of its roof burned away and never replaced, hay stacked in the covered part, Ian, in the cool darkness, while sun ran like water into the open side, swam in the bales, jumped from one layer to another, wriggled between them, hid. Yellow seed popped into the air as he played, and each time he buried himself he came back up with more long stalks on his short-sleeved shirt and his arms. He chanted to himself, "Don-ta-don," rolling and sidling, pulling hay away with his hands, then heaping it back over himself, "Don-ta-don." He said, "Don-ta-don," and was a diving thing, a creature of animal strength and warlike thrusts which hid and then revealed itself; fearless, it nevertheless sought the lower bales and the spaces between them nearest to the floor. And when the smell of strong cigarettes came up the dirt path behind the barn on the hillside, and when Brenda's voice came, singing hoarsely and low, the creature went to ground.

She pulled a bale out by its strings and laid it along her right shoulderblade and flank. Bursting up from cover, the hiding thing called, "Yah-*hah*!" Brenda straightened, took the cigarette from her mouth as she eased the bale back down, said quietly, "Ian, I have asked you not to muck about in the hay. Now you come down off of there and help me scatter this to the rubbishy creatures, will you?"

She stooped under the bale, got it up again and, the cigarette in her mouth, walked away behind the barn. Ian followed her, his arms against his sides, shedding his camouflage, leaving a trail.

In their cottage, Ian's father arranged his sticks on the wide slate fireplace around the circular brazier. He had tiny twigs on the right, against the plaster wall, then larger twigs that were thin, then small branch pieces, then pieces of sapling that he and Ian had dragged down from the hillside forest behind the houses, then round rough pieces of rotten tree that were almost dry and might burn. He had a bucket of coal chunks, and wrinkled pages of *The Times*. Around some paper, he laid the littlest sticks. Stuart put a piece of sapling on while Ian's mother sat on the wide old couch and drank whiskey from a teacup. Ian sat next to his mother, his knees a little together, his eyes on his father, but his mouth a bit open, as if he thought of something else.

Ian's father said, "No, Stuart!"

Ian's mother said, "Come here, Stu."

Stuart pushed another piece of wood into the tepee shape and his father said, "*Stu*art!"

Ian's mother said, "Come here, Stu."

Ian's father said, "Would you mind getting him, Anna? If you want me to make this damned thing."

She said, "I didn't ask for the fire, Harry. If it's too much of a mess with Stuart around, let's skip it. I don't care."

Ian said, "Can I match the fire, Mommy? Can I light the match?"

His mother said, "Ask your father. He handles the hearth and home."

His father stood up, looked at her, then at Ian, squatted down again in front of the slate shelf and said, "Come on, Ian, before the monster strikes again." Ian stood beside his father, held the yellow box of Swan Vestas, then opened it and took one, started to scratch it alight, then stood again, his hands at his sides, as his father took the box, closed it, handed him the single match and the box, and said, "Okay, my friend, light us up."

Ian struck toward himself. His father held his hand and showed him to strike away. Ian tried it three times, and on the fourth the match lit. He dropped the yellow box, stepped backward, then moved himself to the paper and twigs, bent down, singed his fingers, dropped the match into the metal grate, and closed his eyes. His father held the finger inside the circle of his fist, then kissed the finger, picked up the yellow box and handed it back. Ian took out a match, closed the box, struck, struck, lit the match, stooped to the fireplace, singed his finger, dropped the lighted match onto the paper, which caught, and then he stood again to be held by his father's fist while the paper roared, burnt the small sticks up, and everything went out.

His mother said, "It almost did it."

Ian said, "I lit it all right, didn't I?"

His father said, "You did fine. I built it wrong."

His mother said, "I love you."

Ian turned. He said, "Who?"

In his white jockey shorts and undershirt, his long feet bare, Ian moved in the house while swallows called outside and the morning warmed. He opened the door from the stairs to the main room and watched his father, under heavy gray wool blankets on the couch, rolling slowly in his sleep as if his sleep were sea.

His father's mouth was open, and Ian moved closer to look inside. Then he went back to the door and upstairs silently, and he stood at Stuart's cot. The quilt was off, and Stuart's bottom stuck into the air above his gathered knees, mouth closed, face wholly still. Ian went on his toes to the double bed his mother slept in, her mouth open, her brows bunched into lines. He waited, and then he went on his toes again down the stairs and silently to the little refrigerator for apples and the table loaf and the long sharp knife. He heard his father say, "Ian?"

Ian said, "I'm making breakfast for everyone, Daddy. I'm making enough."

On the trekking path through the moors they criss-crossed with sheep tracks, going over one, then another, then descending later to the first, the horses walking around great gray lumps of wrinkled granite and cliffs of slate and later on, delicate hooves under rolling round bodies, slowly dancing over a fast beck that ran in a deep narrow valley for a mile. On the sheep track over the valley, and with the sheep above and below them, shaggy, turd-smeared, expressionless, terrified in place but hungry enough not to move, they rode: Brenda first, her small silver earrings pitching light, then the grandfather, then Ian's father behind him, then Ian, holding the edge of the saddle and leaning onto the pony's neck. Behind him were the long stretches of swamp and thick green grass, the little bolls of fell cotton where the water was murkiest on the surface, and the distances back to the cottage where his mother and Stuart were alone.

Ian's grandfather rode high and straight-backed, his toes pushing in his black pointed boots back against his horse's motion. Ian's father bobbed like a toy rider on a toy horse. Ian held on. Brenda rode ahead, then waited near a cluster of junipers, gray-brown and tense on the sky. When the other riders reached her, Brenda let her horse move out ahead again a little quickly, and Ian's grandfather's horse went too, more quickly than the others. Ian's father pulled on the reins and slowed, and Ian and his father went one behind the other, slowly, over the ridge of junipers, until they caught up to the others at the wide clear tarn where Brenda's white and gray horse was drinking, and where the grandfather looked toward them and then turned his back. As they came up, Brenda said to Ian, "There's tadpoles in there. You want to have a look before we go—if your father thinks it's all right. Walk in shallow and mind you don't slip."

Ian's father smiled, and Brenda helped Ian down, and he waded in, slipping on the wet stones and slimy vegetation. Brenda drove the horses back away from the water and tied them away from the yews, which she said they could die from eating. She gave Ian's father a cigarette and she lit it for him. Ian, in the water to his ankles, teetering, watched.

Brenda said, "Will you all be going home, then, Harry?"

She blew smoke out. Ian heard it over her teeth.

His father said, "Anna's the one who knows that."

Ian stood in the cold mountain lake and watched a black bird hanging in the wind, not moving much.

The grandfather said, "I think you've got some ground to cover yet, Harry."

Ian watched. He saw Brenda blow smoke out through her teeth and throw the cigarette into the water. He saw the grandfather watch it float.

In the parking lot behind the Church Inn, near the small iron tables, Ian, in his shorts and Wellingtons, squatted at a mound of gravel in front of his grandfather's Morris

Minor estate wagon. With the edges of his hands, Ian channeled and heaped the stones. His father drank from a pint of bitter and his mother drank whiskey. Ian put a stick in the center of the mound, then made a double line of little rocks which led toward the center. He ran a little green steel Land Rover back and forth on his road. His parents stood and talked, and closer to the whitewashed walls of the inn Brenda and the grandfather sat at a table.

Ian's mother said, "Dad's going to get in trouble. He really doesn't know."

Ian's father said, "Oh. I thought they were already—you know."

His mother said, "No, she has a room there, in a sort of a separate wing upstairs. It opens into the hallways of the cottage. She lives there and mostly cooks for herself. Sometimes she eats with him, but that's all."

"Are you sure?"

"Poor Daddy. He's sixty-five, going on twenty-five, and it won't work for him."

"She's quite a girl."

"You noticed."

Ian pushed a large rock with the Land Rover and it fell onto the fence he'd made for his road. He pushed the pebbles back with the edges of his hands, then started again to move the stone. A waitress came out with red terrycloth table mats to hang on the washline nearby, and Ian's parents smiled to her. Ian kept working. He heard his father say, "I noticed you. You and the kids. That's what I came over here for."

At the tables behind the public room the grandfather sneezed. He choked one, and then two fast shouts came after, like shots. Ian stood up to look past the clothesline and over low hedges. The grandfather was talking to Brenda, rubbing the sleeve of his brown tweed coat.

After Brenda had shoveled and swept, had stacked the push broom and shovel and rake, and had put the wheelbarrow away, Ian went into the stone stable and closed the double doors behind him. The walls were whitewashed halfway around, and the opposite doors, leading into the field with its small stream, were open, so that cool winds and the white clean stones of the walls made everything smell good. The gelding, the oldest and largest of the horses, dark brown and dull in the shadows of his wooden stall, ate and blew out; the noise of his feeding was a river sound. Ian smelled the ammonia and the hay of the horses, and he breathed deeply. He heard the horses in the field, and he heard his mother.

She said, "Ian?"

Ian said, "Hello."

"Hello."

Ian said, "Are we going home to America?"

"Where's that?"

Brenda lit Ian's father's cigarette and threw the wooden match onto the cobbles in front of the cottage. Ian sat inside on the wooden windowseat and watched, and his mother, on the sofa between him and the room, facing in, sat with a heavy book that Ian's grandfather had given her. She read while Stuart played with coal from the scuttle. The rain was heavy, and Brenda wore her duffel coat with the hood up, but Ian's father wore only his sweater with the reindeer on it as they shoveled and swept inside the stables, then loaded the muck and wheeled it out to the lower stable where they sometimes kept foals.

Stuart spat out a small piece of coal, and Ian's mother lit a cigarette, holding it in her mouth with one hand, working the match back and forth with the other. Beyond her was Ian, who looked at her and then out at the rain beating into the cobbles, and his father helping Brenda with her work, and then the fence and five slow horses wheeling silently from pile of hay to pile, in their dance.

Ian watched everything. He saw his grandfather go down the walk from the house, come around past where the cars were parked, then walk on the cobbles in his leather shoes that clicked, the collar of his brown tweed jacket up against the rain, his gray hair soaking onto his head, showing only pink there by the time he'd knocked on their door and walked in.

The grandfather said, "That child is eating coal." He shut the door, turned his collar down, opened his buttons, rebuttoned them, shook his arms in place at his sides, walked into the middle of the small room to stop where he looked at Ian's mother and, behind her, at Ian, who turned around and pulled his knees up and held them in place with his hands. "Is it good for him? Large pieces like that?" Stuart held the coal up to the grandfather, who was looking at Ian's mother.

She said, "No, Daddy. Pick him up, then."

Ian's grandfather picked Stuart up, and Stuart tried to rub the coal into his grandfather's smooth face. But he stopped when his grandfather snarled and shook him in his arms. The grandfather said, "I've been thinking about you and your family, Anna. I've decided what *I* think is best. God knows you haven't been asking but I want to tell you something. I've wanted to give you some sort of advice for weeks. Before your Harry came to retrieve you."

The mother said, "It sounds like I'm a stick. Or a dead duck."

His grandfather said, "And he's a game dog? Ah. No. No. But for some time. Thinking about this." He put Stuart down, and Stuart rubbed his coal into his grandfather's green twill pants. The grandfather slowly kicked at him as he spoke. "I didn't know you smoked anymore, Anna."

Ian's mother said, "We're all taking it up these days."

His grandfather said, "Ah. *There* we're in tune. What we say now rhymes, in a manner of speaking. I mean to say that while I'd prefer *not* to say it, because I hate to sound as much of a fool as I often am, I nevertheless know what you mean. Which is why I've been thinking so much about—it."

Ian's mother patted the end of her cigarette into a small brass ashtray on the sofa. She said, "You're a sexy old pig, aren't you?"

The grandfather nodded. He rubbed his nose. He said, "It's best for all of us in the family that your family be whole. And home. In the States. Don't you agree?"

Ian's mother said, "I've thought that. Couldn't you tell, really? No, you couldn't tell. You were busy counting your hormones. Old pig. But I've thought about it. It's impossible to tell someone. Like this. In a situation like this. To have the courage or blandness to say: Let's take this awkward and embarrassing and slightly hopeless situation and—whatever you do say." His mother shook her head.

The grandfather put his hands in his sportcoat pockets, then took his right hand out to rub the tip of his nose back and forth. He slowly pushed the toe of his pebbly bright brown shoe into Stuart's stomach as Stuart rubbed a piece of coal along his trouser bottoms. He said, "Right. I suppose it's time to lay claim. Try to." He pushed the back of his hand into his nose, and Ian's mother stood up and leaned her fingers on the front of his dark brown shirt. The grandfather said, "Do I represent the family honor handsomely?" Ian's mother nodded. Her mouth was down and tight, as if she held a cigarette between her lips. Ian's grandfather asked, "Do you think the family is in senile decay?" He rubbed his nose. Then he went to the door and outside.

The day's rain had made the stables cold, and Brenda had left the lights off while she and Ian's father did the mucking out. Ian's mother said, "Why don't you wait in the house, love?" But Ian backed against a stall post and stood there, watching his father hold a cigarette in his mouth. Brenda lighted her own and threw the wooden match onto the cobbled floor. The grandfather moved to step on it, and Ian's mother moved back and so did Brenda. Ian's father stepped around toward him, stopped on the other side of the stall, and then they all waited.

The grandfather said, "Put out that silly cigarette."

Ian's father and Brenda said, "Me?"

Ian's mother laughed. Stuart moved against her and she shifted him to her other side. She said, "Brenda, I'm going to write to you. All right?"

Brenda, in the corner where the tools stood, stared at Ian's mother, then said, "Don't expect me to write back. I can hardly spell me name. And I can't testify that you'll have the address right by then."

The grandfather crossed his arms on his chest, shivered, ducked his head down, closed his eyes, and belched the sneezes out. Ian saw his mother close her eyes and shake her head. Then the grandfather sneezed onto his arm and pressed his arm against his nose. The gelding backed out, then moved again toward the front of his stall. Ian's grandfather sneezed again, and the gelding came out fast, a hoof stabbing, then banging onto the cobblestones, stabbing back. Ian stayed where he was, leaning against the post. Brenda said, "Get out," very softly as she walked so smoothly she seemed to be skating on ice instead of lifting floppy boots. She said, "Everybody move slowly. Get out."

Ian's mother said, "Ian."

His father came across the circle with his arm out.

The grandfather sneezed into both of his hands.

Ian stood against the post.

Brenda said, "Get out now. Everybody get out."

THE OLD MAN

IS SNORING

Nov. 7   New mailman today. Tom Lavaca said to say hello. Talked about Tom's retirement, postal wages, etc. New man also named Tom, last name Pimento. Query: Do Italians dominate certain postal zones? Flyer from cut-rate store, letter from Tri-State Electric re leak in their meter (they say I'm wrong, their bills right), bill from pharmacy. Also alumni bulletin. Query: Are more members of the division who survived the war dying of old age or of accidents? Response: It *feels* like age, probably is: end of a generation. Out for cigarettes and paper. Library: Ngaio Marsh, new Michael Gilbert. Wonder if Gilbert wears mustache. Lunch: half can tuna, glass

Calif. wine w/water, lettuce. (Lettuce up from last week.) Made appointment with Dr. Katz. Query: When I retired we had six MDS in town, now we have one. Does town decline *because* people leave it or *as* they do? Dinner: drumstick, wine w/water, salad, tea. Tv. Cold night, high winds, no snow. Early bed.

N o v. 8   Woke early but stayed under covers. Query: Origin of "undercover"? Response: Doubtful. Didn't want breakfast but had some: tea, toast, marmalade. Long walk (Ribbon Hill Rd. farm). Foot still bad. Met Tom Pimento. Funny eyes. Troubled man? Reminded me of Negro outfit near Ljubljana. Their major (white man), after white machine-gunners in support unit fired on blacks, killed twenty (more?). Major kept saying accident, sure ("show"—Southern). Eyes kept saying otherwise. Tom Pimento, sad man. Long nap, slept through lunchtime, wakened by phone. Billy Webb wanted to borrow soldering iron, said sure. Answered letter from Tri-State, paid pharmacy bill, read *Popular Science* (came today). Larraine Belding over to say hello. Says can't get used to living alone. Told her time heals, was embarrassed, didn't know what else to say. Unseasonal snowstorm: told her to stay for tea, made fire in fireplace. Pleasant. Dinner: broiled frozen trout, water, lettuce, etc. Speculated about freezing individual salads in broth or gel (keep leaves stiff) which would melt off upon defrosting. Would need plastic dish with drain holes for broth to drip into. Ugly. Soggy. Finished Michael Gilbert, fell asleep in chair. Wakened by plows going past, their chains. Bed.

N o v. 9   Letter addressed to Margaret. Sat with it. Wondered whether it should be opened. Query: Should postal service include automatic transfer of dead people's mail to their survivors' attorney? Response: Too expensive. And survivors might want the mail *sometimes*. Letters to dead people—like their ghosts. Her freshman-year roommate sends announcement of her husband's death. Thought it quite funny. When Tom Pimento gave me the letter, his eyes looked bad again. Might be too young to be a postman. Galoshes, sweaters, jacket, the old camouflage coat (but white side in, so plow drivers can see the khaki), grand walk into center of town. Paper, cigarettes, lunch at the hotel. Glass of wine with old Royce Hudson. Looked very bad, says loses balance all the time. Made jokes (*mental* balance, etc.) but sad occasion. Enjoyed walk home, though foot a nuisance. Wrote part of membership-drive letter for alumni bulletin. Mentioned those *Alpini* who gave us their mountain hats at end of war. Quite moving. Dinner: chicken slices, tea, salad, etc. Watched President's news conference. Wouldn't let him pack my parachute. Bed.

N o v. 1 o Letter from new principal: Would I give an informal talk in June to graduating students. Called up, said delighted, etc. Query: Why do I think of pomade when I hear his voice? Response: My jealousy? Maybe. He is slick. But bright boy. Be all right. Snow melting off. Shouldn't be here to begin with. Call from Larraine Belding: Could we spend Thanksgiving together, doesn't want to be alone on family holiday, etc. Told her Teddy and Una usually do something and want me with them. We'll see, etc., won't forget her, etc. Sounds god-awful lonely. Must drop by. Walked for cigarettes and paper. Bus with newspapers late (again!). Tea at hotel. Georgie Dubermann there, says he hates retirement. Query: Government Job Corps for retired people? Response: Something like it exists, but they take businessmen and let them read to blind people. Georgie needs *work*. Everyone, probably. Papers came at eleven. Read *Register* at hotel. Wonder if we need so many submarines. Query: Why not smuggle H-bombs into foreign capitals, assemble and hide them in fused casings (detonate if tampered with), then announce this to world? Invite Russia, etc., to do same here. Balance of terror. Then use submarine and bomber money for hospitals, etc.? Tunafish, wine w/water for lunch. Long nap. Woke at three, made fire, worked on membership letter. Thought of time I had two kids detailed to me and we guarded wine warehouse until colonel's truck arrived. So drunk, we wet our pants! Lambchop, salad, small glass wine for dinner. *Bad Day at Black Rock* on TV. Tracy my idea of a man, one arm or not. Rain during night. Out of bed to watch it freeze on streets.

Nov. 11   The anniversary. Brought Sunday *Times* with me. Decided on Methodist church (Bill Terman's). Enjoyed the singing. Said to myself during sermon, Well, Margaret, here I am in the fourth year without you. Left. Read magazine section in hotel—peculiar boy who plays chess, emerging nations. Two cups of tea. Book review section: angry feminist attacking male homosexual novel for "plagiarizing" female characteristics. Didn't think she showed much compassion. Splendid-sounding crime novels—new Peter Dickinson. Read news-review section about President's obvious scandal involvement. Tom Lavaca joined me (wife at RC services). Said President guilty, but what to do, etc. Pointed out Dr. Katz: quiet little man, funny small mustache, bow tie. Tom said Katz's son arrested for smuggling drugs from Bizerte to Italy to Switzerland. Caught in Bern. Sad. Had short leave in Bern once, visiting Cousin Willie in hospital. Horrible city, good beer, I think. Saw Katz's wife: stout woman with mustache like husband's. Carried old miniature schnauzer under arm. Tom agreed re Tom Pimento. Maybe too young for responsibilities, but nice boy. Wife and kids. Tom (Lavaca) thinking of moving to Florida—warmer, etc. Miss him if he goes. Treat for lunch: grilled cheese sandwich (cholesterol!) and glass of beer. Very exciting football games, watched for two or three hours. Built fire. Called Larraine Belding. Still sad. Started Ngaio Marsh: so-so. Dinner: fish sticks, tiny bit of rice, no wine, large salad. Read the Marsh—Roderick Alleyn okay, wife too sensitive. Radio says snow, feels like it. Much too early in year. Early bed.

N o v. 1 2 Dreamed of Margaret. Not surprising. Query: Could psychiatrists prepattern patients' dreams as part of therapy? Also dreamed of snow, all around the house, heaping over it. Frightening. Can't remember the one about Margaret. Just as well. Letter from Teddy: they're going to Una's parents in NJ. Good idea, she hasn't seen them for months. Called Larraine Belding, no answer. Cigarettes and paper, stopped at pharmacy to chat with Bob Fisher. Home with flu (saw his wife). Limping now on the damned foot. Some kind of callus on heel? Blister? Funny cartoon on editorial page, clipped it. Wonder who writes jokes. Once heard it was teletype operators with nothing to do at night, talking to each other. Idea for a book: people who work at night. A different world. Library: ordered new Peter Dickinson, new Alistair Maclean, took out early Ross Macdonald (usu-

ally better than newer stuff) and Robert Heinlein's *Sixth
Column*. Walked to Grand Union after leaving off books.
Too noisy, bright. Woman still stares at me when I pack
groceries into knapsack. Each to his own, madam. Bottle of wine from Walter's: like the way he's always cheerful. Lunch: half can of tuna, salad (lettuce up again!),
wine w/water. Nap in chair. Woke up sweating. Bad
dreams? Can't remember. Just as well. Called Larraine
Belding, no answer. Called Teddy and Una as surprise.
No answer. Worked on membership letter. Looking forward to alumni dinner. Finished tuna, little rice, no wine
for dinner. Monday night football game on TV: O. J.
Simpson! Bed, high winds at windows.

Nov. 13 Couldn't sleep. Did what I did when I ran the
business: reviewed problems so time wouldn't be wasted.
Couldn't think of problems to review. Got itchy, angry.
Too cold to get out of bed. Read the Heinlein. US taken
over by Asians. Heroes go underground. Led by reserve
officer, advertising man. Long time since ad man was a
hero in this country! President filled gov't. with them.
Not a good idea. Lawyers corrupt also. Billy Graham
and that Jesuit ditto. Next President should hire men
with small businesses. Harry Truman. Could use him now.
Ike. Fell asleep late. Dreamed about snow again. All over
the house, breaking the windows. Woke early. Big breakfast, long walk in snow for cigarettes and paper. Mailed
off handwritten draft of alumni letter. Met Tom Pimento
on way. Said no mail for me. Touched my shoulder, said
sorry. Funny eyes. I said it wasn't that bad, was it? Joke.
Tom didn't understand. Wonder if he's all right. Postal
rates up again. Service certainly slower. Sign of the times.
Query: Use retired people for special delivery? They

could work for less money, would enjoy the travel, meeting people, etc. Maybe same-day delivery service. Response: Let just one die in the middle of a delivery—would give the service a black eye. Hope the membership drive works. Lunch: poached egg, toast, margarine, tea. Sneaked some fig bars for dessert. Foot hurt, put it up, read *Register*. Terrible airplane crash in Japan. Hope Ted and Una don't fly to NJ. Take train. Query: Are trains declining because people don't use them, or do people stay away from them because trains are declining? Oil embargo, clever weapon. Wonder why they hate the Jews so much. Georgie Dubermann an old Jew, German—thoroughly decent man. Going to die soon. Called Larraine Belding, told her we could have Thanksgiving together. She's flying to Boston for TG with old friends. Do her good. Dr. Katz at 4:15. Very strange. Reception room like hunting lodge: animal heads, knives, matchlock rifle, etc. Woman with dark blue hair asked me questions. Made me feel like I was in bishop's anteroom. First question: Religion. Very strange. Like hospital. In case you need last rites. Many questions, didn't like it. Didn't like self—too dutiful w/answers. Then Dr. Katz: smaller than I thought. Little arms in short-sleeved shirt. Hot office. One desk light, couldn't see well. Read my form. Looked at me: little eyes, big eyeglasses. Stripped. Heart, lungs, blood pressure. Asked how much I smoked. Stoop, bend over, lie down—didn't like it. Then lying face down on table. Turns out foot had plantar wart in heel. Katz whistling all the time (between teeth). Held ankle, grabbed scalpel from table—definitely *not* sterilized. No anesthetic. Dug into heel. Held table. Resolved not to whimper. Didn't. Did have to ask for rest. Katz went ahead screwing scalpel into heel. Whistled.

Put my head down hard. Katz stopped. Said it was deep. Changed mind re treatment. Put Band-Aid on, no antiseptic! Told me how to soak foot. Thought about his son in jail in Switzerland. Sitting in office again, dressed, Katz looking over low desk lamp at me. Said he had plantar wart in service. Asked where he served—Yugoslavia too! Turned out he served with field hospital attached to us. Takes divisional alumni letter, etc. Whistled, no smile: stared at me. Wouldn't talk old times, didn't ask any questions re war. Gave me *Reader's Digest* reprint, how to stop smoking with yoga. Sat down again, looked at me. Said this softly: "Have you ever thought very seriously about committing suicide?" Funny reaction: made me want to cry. Shook my head no. Asked how much. Charged me twelve. Took two off when I paid cash. Limped home. Foot very bad. Cereal and milk for dinner. Finished Heinlein. Good guys won. Power of advertising. Snow. Early bed.

N o v. 1 4   Called Ted at 8 AM to catch him before he left for work. Forgot they're an hour earlier. Everyone there sleepy, confused. Asked him not to fly to NJ, take train. Suggested plans for Xmas. Strange conversation. No breakfast—tea. Very tired. Plows clanking in streets all night. Dressed for high winds, snow. Waited on porch for Tom Pimento. Said he thought I should stay inside in foul weather. Funny boy. Fuel bill. Note from Bill Terman: Saw me in church on Sunday, was I thinking of regular attendance, did I want to chat some time, etc. Walked for cigarettes and paper. Wondered if Ross Winkler would like membership letter. Good man, Ross. My favorite captain. Used to promise us he'd keep us alive. Believed him every time. No *Register*. Bus couldn't get through. Foot very sore. Hotel for tea. No one else there. Home, more tea, Ross Macdonald (*Zebra-Striped Hearse*). Pea soup for lunch, watched news, soap operas on TV. Made fire, slept on sofa. Woke up frightened. Called Dr. Katz, not in. Woman (blue hair) wouldn't say where he was. Asked her if he was all right. She laughed, hung up. Remembered it was Wed., MDS always off on Wed. PMS. Query: Why do they all take the same day off? Shouldn't one of them stay on duty for emergencies? Then take Thurs. off? Wonder if Katz is really MD. Stories about imposters serving communities as MDS for years. Hope they're better with feet than Katz. Tom Pimento at door with *Register*, bus finally got through. Thoughtful boy. Asked him in for tea, coffee, beer. Kept coat on, sat near fire, talked, drank can of beer, left. Eyes very nervous. Watched me. Made me think of Katz. Asked if house was warm enough. Very young. Ross Macdonald. Pea soup, scrambled eggs, salad, wine w/water. Tv movie: Gary Cooper, Jean Arthur. More snow predicted. Bed.

N o v. 1 5   Dreamed I had letter from Margaret. More snow. No mail, Tom Pimento waved. Walked for cigarettes and paper. Papers not in. Tea at hotel. Tomato soup for lunch. Library: Rex Stout, Gavin Lyall. Long nap. Read *Three Men Out*. Liver, onions, wine w/water. No salad. Tv. Bed.

N o v. 1 6   Very cold. Frozen snow, crusts. Foot okay, still sore. Oatmeal. Card from library: Peter Dickinson. Walked in street—sidewalks slippery. Cigarettes and paper. Picked up Dickinson. Tea at hotel. Tom Lavaca— definitely going to Florida. Miss him. Napped through lunch. Ate salad of lettuce and tomato, onion rings. Tea. Read *Register*—Vice President (former) analyzed: petty corruption. Finished *Three Men Out*. Watched TV. Dinner: turkey breast, peas, tea. No salad. Started *Lizard in the Cup*. Sad. Snow. Bed.

N o v. 1 7   Blizzard. No chance of papers. Tried to remember dreams. Tom Pimento late. Ad from Montgomery-Ward. Query: Why most junk mail on Saturdays? Wrote letter to Teddy and Una. Apologized for strange behavior. Lunch: minestrone, roll, wine w/water. Tom Pimento at door: pack of cigarettes. Worried about me walking in storm. Asked him in, wouldn't come. Strange boy. Long nap. College football games on TV: California—sunshine, girls in small skirts. Storm worse. Read Dickinson, mournful old detective. Depressing. Dinner: turkey hash, salad, tea. Tv: John Wayne—hundreds of people beaten, shot. Started Lyall, *Venus with Pistol*. High winds. Bed.

N o v. 1 8   Called Dr. Katz. Recording said he was in church. Plows all morning. Woke me last night. Dreams. Oatmeal. Out of cigarettes. Bundled for storm. Walked for cigarettes and paper. Walked to Baptist church, then Methodist. Didn't see Katz. Lutheran church too far, foot not good. Rc? Home. *Times*. Soup, cheese sandwich, wine. No salad. Finished *Venus*. Fell asleep in chair. Nightmares. Plows. Bed.

N o v. 1 9   Dreamed of war. Glad to wake up. Breakfast: fried egg, tea. Foot fine. Met Tom Pimento on porch. Clapped him on shoulder. Stared at me. *National Geographic*. Went for cigarettes and paper. Called on

Larraine Belding. Tea. Cheerful. Returned library books, checked out Thomas B. Dewey (*Don't Cry for Long*), Rex Stout (*League of Frightened Men*). Home. Ham slice, salad, wine w/water. Called Dr. Katz. Woman w/blue hair put me through. Didn't know what to say to him. Said yes. He didn't know what I meant. Sounded angry. Waited. Asked if he? Quiet both ends. Hung up. Wine. Nero Wolfe and Archie. Dinner: open grilled cheese sandwich, salad, wine. Wondered about marrying Larraine Belding. Won't marry anyone. Tv: Monday night football game—Giants dreadful, announcers scornful. No snow. Streets quiet. Bed.

IS

ANYONE LEFT

THIS TIME OF

YEAR?

Not in Wexford, not in Cork. Not in Limerick, nor Nenagh, Killalo, Tulla, Gort. Nor Galway, under the Spanish arch on slimy cobbles near the bay where gypsy children beg. And not in Oughterard, the clap of crowding Galway gone, the smell of so many hungry breaths. And then there is Clifden. You can drive yourself deeper into the west if you want. You can get yourself nearly into the sea, rip the oil pan out on rocks and scours down to Aughrus More or Kill. But Clifden is far enough, coming in at dusk past the Twelve Bens and the autumn bogs of purple and burnt-brown that go like tide flats away from the cracked road's edge. You keep on driving west at the low red sun and fall into Clifden like a suitcase loaded with stones that falls in the sea.

The Dromaneen is closed. The Ivy Manor is closed. Salt House is closed. Keogh's is closed. The long dark street of Clifden runs to the other long street; they meet at a very sharp angle and point down the hill, over the brick and mortar ruins of the Old Town, over moss-grown steps and broken paving, into the bay. Paper and cans swept from bins by the wind are in the streets, moving. Light from the car shows where on the streets the car, swept in from the east, is moving too. Empty metal kegs of Harp and Guinness crowd the curbings every three doorways and then there is light from the Metropolitan, open, and the light falls onto the street and MAUMEEN'S —HIGH CLASS VICTUALLER. UNDERTAKER. Closed. The Alcock and Brown is open; this is tinted glass and white stone and Connemara marble labeled CONNEMARA MARBLE. This is where the red and brown tour buses come, where the lobby is rich with Irish coffee and genuine Irish wool and the booklets on Alcock and Brown, who ended their transatlantic airplane race by landing at Lough Fadda in a bog at an angle of forty-five degrees, sinking.

I land at the Inishturk Hotel, which is always open in the early fall, though most of the tourists are home or at the Alcock and Brown. I come from the dark clenched street past the foyer, where they still have not covered the red and black circuits and switches and fusebox plates that crawl on the high left-hand wall like a network of nerves. And there is the white urn of umbrellas, the bright brass handle on the door to the fireplace room, the Irish china and African hangings and red-flowered wallpaper, hundred-year-old wood of steps and bannister that go up to three floors of rooms. There is the dark carpet that goes past the desk with Peter O'Toole's signature under glass into the empty cavernous unlit lounge—vases and candlestands and feathers on lampshades, the wood of dried arrangements, ebony, Waterford crystal, ugly prints in golden frames. The emptiness, silence, absorption of light: what you drive at the sun for, fall to from lichenous mountains, Clifden, *An Clochan*, The Stepping Stones.

If I didn't come at the dusk of a Sunday past silent men who curl forever on donkey chaises, rocked, staring down their cigarettes at the road, and then past only the black road and darkening bogs, I could go down the hill to a ramp where cattle graze above the sea and seem, at a distance and when the sun is bright on the water, to step on the ocean and eat. But at night now I can enter the empty hotel and be noticed in a while and fill in the form and give the registration code and passport number and forwarding address—write *None*—and wait for Sheila to look and smile with her beaked angry nose, eyes with still too much of the dark silver makeup around them, and say, "Oh, *now* so. Of course. You didn't come again yet. We wondered, weeks back. So now you're here. And I've given a single one to you! That's easy to change, this time of year."

And then I must tell her to leave it at a single room.

And she must say, "Oh. A single, then."

And I must say a single, then.

She must look away, to Peter O'Toole's modest hand. Then she: "Well, I'll take you up myself, then, if you've no objections. You of all should know how there's nearly no one left this time of year. We do it all ourselves, you'll remember. Mother and me. We shall perish if we don't take care, I suppose. Overwork even in November, to listen to us."

I follow her dark short skirt, bright thighs, up the carpeted stairs to Room Eleven, its dense rich blankets and rug, the squat Victorian bureau, high wardrobe from some other time, the electric fire with ragged cord, the window over the street and the coastal perfume of mildew barely contained, and the usual slatted folding rack on which one lays his suitcase filled with stones.

She says, "We're happy you're back and dinner is always half-seven."

I tell her I'm happy I'm back, and dinner at half-seven.

She says, "I remember now all your jokes about my marrying at thirty-three, you know. Well, this year I'm thirty-four." She smiles her angry smile and holds her naked fingers out, like a child in school, for inspection. "Will you tell me *this* is the lucky year?"

Then there is the room and what is in it and the time to wait. Then, still waiting, there is the private bar downstairs, the light-stained wood, bright fabrics, low uncomfortable chairs against the walls, the round china ashtrays and white plastic lightshades and Sheila behind the bar, who draws the Guinness but this time doesn't smile.

Her mother in tinted glasses who is six feet tall is smoking short cigarettes on the customers' side of the bar, telling her stories again to the ladies. One, in an open raincoat, leans back low in her straight-back chair and watches her hands on the cocktail table snap a little lighter on and off. Smoke from a frayed butt goes up in a line from her ashtray out of sight. Another lady, in a red plaid tailored suit, sits straight on a high square barstool and stares ahead, out of sight, and nods. The inside of her wrist leans on her collarbone and her fingers hold the cigarette near her lips and she squints inside of its smoke and stares. They have all together done their hair, which is knotted on the nape and parted in the middle, drawn back very tight, very blue.

Sheila's mother puffs and leans against the bar and tells her story of Murray who won a what-you-may-call-it, *letter*, in swimming in the States. Murray is about to dive from their drifting gondola into the reeking Venetian canal. And she is about to ask the gondolier if he can swim. Then she is going to hold her question, for what if he can't? When she can't either, and at her age and condition of life? And Murray is about to dive and slide, like a pale freckled porpoise, through the stinking waters, then climb back into the boat and shiver and grin. They are about to head back. She is about to learn that the gondolier cannot swim. She will come to say, " 'Our sweet sacred Mother' is what I said. 'And that *still* don't make me your sister, you Roman,' I said," she will say, and they will laugh.

I go out to the dark still lobby and leave them poised —the boy on the hired gunwale, the mother in fear at the Romish canal—and stand in the empty fireplace lounge, with its coal fire silent and reeking; everything metal or wooden is polished, and shapes come back from all around in the coal's low light.

When Sheila comes in, there is only the hiss of coal and the falling of ash through the grate. You of all should know how there's nearly no one left this time of year. Then she puts the half-gone glass of stout on the imitation-ivory-inlaid table near the door and does not look away from what she does and is out of the writhing reflections and the sound of ash gone down. We do it all ourselves, you'll remember. We shall perish if we don't take care.

The small gold cymbal at the stairs' first turning is rung. Twenty-five tables covered with white are in the room, long and oval and sheeted and cold. Five long tables are covered with glassware and silver that crowds to every edge, and there is a bright red paper napkin at each place, and lights above each loaded table, hot on the ceiling, cold and yellow below. One of the tables has napkins and glasses and plates at each place, but silverware at only one, and Sheila sees me to the seat. She says, "I thought it would make for more cheer. We haven't that many people, you know. Two others, only. They're just married. They showed me how Hallowe'en is played in the States. We played Bob o' the Apple and we caught ghosts and lighted a squash. There's only one meal on the menu this time of year, you'll remember. Is that all right with you?"

I tell her only one meal on the menu is all right with me this time of year. The darkened rest of the room is like the hall of a closed museum.

Sheila brings what the meal is and takes the dishes away. I thank her after each course. She looks some other place. She says, "Would you like any more? We have enough for more if you'd like." She pulls at the towel tucked into her apron and her hands caress one another as if there is comfort there.

I tell her no and thank her, and she brings the bitter coffee and then takes the cup away. She brings a cognac and goes away and the newly married Americans come. She has hair the color of the red that is shiny on green pears, and he is bald and tall. His face reacts to everything she does and hers, all earnest frowns, reacts to what he says. They are happy with each other through the cheese and biscuits, and then he orders two sweet cherry liqueurs, and she hesitates and shakes her head. Sheila brings me another cognac, and the husband drinks the liqueur. The wife shakes her head again, and he reaches for her glass. Sheila comes with one more cognac, and the husband finishes her drink and orders one more. His wife says, "No more?" She says to Sheila, "We hardly ever drink."

His face goes red. I watch it change as the burn goes across it. But he shakes his head and finally grins, says, "I didn't really want the first one. It tasted like cherry cough medicine at home. We hardly ever drink."

When they leave, he moves her chair back from the table and helps her away. He leans a shoulder, an arm, toward her as if to shield her from something in ambush. She pulls on his sleeve, and he nods, bending down to her, and straightens and turns to me and nods, says, "Well, good night now." She smiles very widely as if she were trying to say something earnest and useful, something more helpful than only good night.

I say good night.

Sheila comes back when the couple is gone and says, "Could I bring you anything more? Aren't they gentle people? Pardon, of course, but especially for Americans. They have all that love on them like rain on a tree."

I ask her for a cognac and thank her.

She wipes her hands on the towel and says, "You know we have to charge you five-and-three for every glass?"

I thank her for worrying.

"I don't mind worrying, then."

I cough and look at the table and wait.

She says, "Did you enjoy the meal?"

I say that I enjoyed the meal. Then I look at the table and then I ask Sheila if she would like to drink a brandy with me.

She says, "Not until you mean that, thank you just the same, and I haven't driven you to it in desperation. I'm sorry that you've felt so."

Her angry eyes are on my face. I tell her that I'm driven to nothing at all. I tell her not to worry, and I smile. She leaves and returns with the cognac, and I tell her maybe we can have a drink before I leave.

"And leaving already?" she says.

I tell her no. I tell her I don't know. I look at the brandy, which is colored in the dim cold light like the stiffened surface of the dying bogs I came through, burnt-away brown and gold all day underneath no sky. It was the color of ashes in all directions, from the ground straight up, with no cloud and no color and no light reflected—dirty ash gone down on everything, and no sky. Through Maam Cross, Recess, and Ballynahinch, I came under no sky, and at Cashel Hill, among the Bens, the day was punctured by dusk, the sides collapsed, and ashen horizons leaked out, and there was the sun: red and swollen, grazing on the surface of the sea. You drive your car down the final hills and at the sun, to Clifden, where you drink the night's last cognac and see that she has gone—so leave the glass on the table and go to bed.

I go to bed. And later, in the dark, I sit up. I sit in the bay of the window and watch the town and sleep there, falling forward and coming out of sleep with my fingers clawing, my lips wide apart and dry, cracking sounds coming up from my sleep which I don't want to hear. Barefoot and in pajamas, I go downstairs along the carpeting to stand, like a child at night in the big house, before the locked saloon bar door. There are no fires and no lights. The flesh of my feet shines phosphorescent, like fishes belly-up in dark waters. I stand and I look at the door and shrug my shoulders and stand.

Sheila's mother says, "Do you need a drink?"

She wears wide-legged white pajamas under a dark robe and she must have dark slippers on, for she looms above me and all I see to hold her up is an inch of white-ness a little over the floor. Her hair is still up, her brown-tinted glasses still on, a cigarette yet in her hand, its redness moving as she speaks. She says, "Do you need a small something?"

I say I need something.

She says, "I do myself. Almost always now."

Her keys ring as if they are huge, and she opens the door in above the inch of whiteness that moves along the floor. She does not turn the bar lights on, but goes behind the counter—it smells like the closet of a dirty smoker, cigarettes and flesh combined—and she serves me some-thing that I drink. She pours it for herself and then for me, and I wrestle up to a stool while she drinks and pours again.

"Isn't it a pity not to sleep?" she says. "I never knew what peace meant until I lost the power of sleep."

I say it is a great pity not to sleep.

"The rooms you leave at night lose their attraction in the morning somehow," she says. "As if they need your sleep to renew them as well as you yourself needing the sleep, sort of. Do you follow me?"

I say I've noticed it also, rooms eroding.

"Do you pray at night?" she says. "Are you re-ligious?"

I say that I am not religious. I say I don't pray.

"Does that mean you have no hope?" she says. "Would you like another?"

I say I don't mind.

"John Jameson," she says. "Not that Old Paddy—which is genuine Irish, right enough, but it's coarse like most of the genuine Irish. *And* a bad bargain, like the genuine Irish, costing as much as a good whiskey does. Have you tasted the difference?"

I say I've tasted them both and Paddy is coarse. I say I don't mind.

She says, "Do you have feelings over the Belfast problems they're having?"

I say no.

She pours us each another, then says, "Is there anything you'd care to discuss, then?"

I say no.

She says, "Then I'll leave you the bottle, and with our good wishes, and I will be off to my bed if not, Lord willing, my sleep."

I thank her and wish her sleep and she is gone. I leave my drink on the bar and walk around the room. Into my eyes, the pupils large enough by now, and focused, things like chairs and ashtrays come, and then they're out and I've gone around the room again. Soon I stop and finish my drink, leave the glass beside the bottle and go outside, closing the door very gently. On the carpeted steps, a blanket around her head and torso, like a gypsy woman sleeping at someone's door a while, squats Sheila; her feet are covered, her arms are in the blanket, so only the low brightness of her face shows up—unappeased eyes and angry beak and teeth.

"I see you're having a difficult night," she says. "Who teased me once about long nights."

I say yes.

"I'm sorry," she says. She says, "Couldn't people ever help each other with their lives?"

I tell her I wouldn't know.

"Shouldn't they do what they can?" she says. "Make the try for comfort's sake?"

I tell her no. I go up past her on the steps and from the back and the stairs' first turning she is vanished into her blanket. She is one of the Inishturk's dark fabrics in the slack season, waiting for another year.

I go to bed and fall asleep and my cracked lips wake me up and then I sleep again. Then it is morning and time for breakfast, which the newlyweds don't attend. Sheila has the electric fires on. She brings in coffee and sets it before me in that ballroom of silence. She folds her towel and says to it, "What can I make you for breakfast?"

I ask her how she slept. She nods and I see the sockets of her eyes, silver shadow gone. I tell her some kind of juice and thank her.

She says, "I made my decision last night. Would you like to hear it?"

I say yes.

She says, "I've decided I'm marrying in the time between when we close and when we open in May. It means I'll be a *missus* if you come here again in the fall and notice me about, laughing and all."

I say good, getting married.

"Because it's time now not to live alone. And mothers don't count in such. It's time now not to be living alone anymore at my time and place."

I look at the table, and then I say yes, that's good, marrying.

"Even if I have to find him in a Galway saloon," she says. "Because I *will* find a husband, I decided now."

I fold my red napkin in quarters and nod. I look at the dark brown sugar, tiny useless teaspoons, the stubs of my fingernails folding the fourths into eighths. I nod and keep nodding while she watches me, and I tell her sausages, tomato, scrambled egg.

Then it is the Brandy and Soda Road, with a sky and sun today before lunch at the Inishturk, saxifrage in the heaths showing, cattle and sheep at the stone fences and in the bogs where the Atlantic pushes through the grass in long tidal pools, like the fingers of a lover in a lover's hair. After a while the bright fading grass is level with the narrow road, and the hills have rippled back to where the sea is.

Past a settlement of three square cement houses, one of which has PROVISIONS neatly painted in black on its wall, an unpaved road curves off and goes behind the houses in a wide brown arc. The houses vanish and a hill comes up, high weeds blown by the wind from the sea. The road, grown rockier, heads for the hill and climbs it, toward three shapes outlined on the sky. A small diesel engine covered by tarps is throbbing; it is surrounded by empty jerry cans used for gasoline; wires from the engine run to a high dark van in which no one is sitting, and antennae on the van's roof jump in the steady hard winds. Nearby is a small blue caravan with padlocked door, the sides scratched deep, the windows covered with blinds. The engine pushes electricity out to the van where the radio is, and no one appears. Down the hill and on the other side is a lower hill, and then the Atlantic foaming in at the bleached-bone sand of the small bay. Out on the ocean there are boats that men here call to with their radio, if the men here call, if there are men to call now, warning of winds such as these that now drive the ocean in and rock the trailer and my car and the untended antennae that the throbbing engine feeds.

It is time to go there now, where the ocean never stops banging onto the bone-white beach, the Shore of the Plover, where the sand is made of tiny shells with nothing in them anymore except the wind.

The dirt road goes down to a narrow track with deep furrows, and the car's sides crush against low weeds and high rocks and the track runs off to the right, away from the bay. There are no houses. There is one long hill to the left, low between the ocean and the track, and then the ground on the right rises up to another low hill, and that comes up near the track, while the fields before the car open out and just go on.

The wheel pulls my hands back and forth, and the steel around me makes sounds of things shaking loose. The light brown earth of the track is disappearing as the car falls farther on. A man is very small with no face on the leftward hill as he lifts from the ground and moves a few steps and then returns to where he was before and stoops and lifts. There is nothing on the hill to my right. And far ahead, down the rock field, at the farthest point of my sight, a small white pony is bent to the ground, and a brown pony stands erect. And the car stops, for the track is gone, and there is only rock and some grass. There is track that stops, and a man who endlessly stoops on top of a hill, and two unmoving ponies down the vast stony meadow, and the track ending, a gash or two in the earth and nothing then: the tiny car, the

tinier man inside it, the hidden sea, the wind, the im-
mensity coming down.

It is time to turn the car around and follow the track
back, pick up the suitcase, and pay them at the Inishturk
and leave, to drive up from Clifden back through the Bens
and east through Maam Cross and Oughterard, across the
Corrib back to see once more if there is someplace, this
time in Galway, down in the crowded small streets, where
someone is left.

SMALL TALK, PRAYERS

Two hundred yards from the boulders and kelp and storm-stranded trees of the upper beach, over the shoulders of the steady grazing Galway cattle and past the Cape Cod house sitting tight and gray against any weather, across the unpaved dead-end road, there is the cottage that the Jews on their summer vacation rent. The windows of the Jews' house are dark. It is Friday night, and they obey arcane injunctions against the switching on of lights. And yet they smear, from time to time, a flicker of candle flame across their blackened windows. They are obedient. They are complex.

In the Cape Cod house of their landlords, there is lemon brightness at the mullioned windows, and a music that cannot be heard without the power of machines. On the Sabbath eve, the Jews will not switch power on. They hear no music. Or perhaps they hear the recordings the Galbraiths play. Who can tell?

Saturday morning, and Mr. Galbraith drives his Volvo away. Long bamboo fishing rods stick out of the windows. At ten o'clock a pale thin child in baggy green shorts emerges from the Jews' house with a little silver gun. He is called back in and shortly reappears unarmed. He heaps gravel in the drive behind his parents' small black Chevrolet, which is dappled with the droppings of bluejays and gulls. Soon he sits, powerless under the bright sun, and contemplates the mounds of small stones.

At ten thirty, a white forty-footer turns in from the line of lobster buoys at the wide cove's entrance and makes toward the crescent of beach. A fog horn is sounded twice, and Mr. Galbraith, short and round, dressed in khakis and a bright white shirt, appears aft as the boat immediately turns to head out to sea. Mr. Galbraith waves toward shore. Mrs. Galbraith, short and slender and dressed as if for a formal meeting or serious shopping, stands in the side yard and waves at the boat. She drives, then, in a long white Buick, down the rutted road toward town. She stops the car, and the child of the Jews, across the road, stands to watch. She waves to him, and he waves back energetically, and then she drives away.

And now it is eleven, and the Jews are walking past their landlords' house, on the trail that runs parallel to the field the Galways graze, and down to the beach. The husband is short and slim and pale, dressed in a white short-sleeved shirt and dark brown trousers rolled to his calves. He wears a yarmulke. He wears blue plastic shower clogs and carries a wicker pack basket on his back. The wife is taller than the husband, also slender. She wears a man's T-shirt and her breasts roll heavily as she walks. Her shoes are ugly and broad, the kind of shoe once known as sensible. Her dark socks puddle at her shoe tops. The child, slightly too small for his large hands and feet, is about seven years old. Twice he picks up sticks that could be thought of as gun-shaped. Twice his mother perceives their possibility, and twice he must throw the sticks down.

The Jews are sporting themselves along the coast of Maine. The mother reads a thick paperback book, and the father lies on a boulder, arms and legs draped down its curves as if he were something deposited by tides. The child is throwing rocks into the Atlantic Ocean. The tide's suck and splash camouflages the drop of each rock. The child sets to rolling heavy logs to the incoming sea. His mother calls to him, and he stops. Soon he starts again, and she watches him, stands as if to call, then sits back against the rocks and reads.

The Jews believe they must not work on Saturday, the Sabbath, or on Friday night, its eve. Turning on electric lights is work. Spending money enables work. Driving a car is work. They neither spend nor drive nor switch on lights. But isn't reading work? Isn't it work to carry a pack to the beach? What of the work involved in restricting a child so that he doesn't play at imaginary murder, itself a form of work? Isn't it work to roll a log into the ocean? Only the father seems to obey in an orthodox sense. Unless he is thinking. His brow is furrowed and his slender lips are down. Is it the sun that curves his features, or does he labor in his brain pan? Clearly, these Jews observe a private religion. Within the framework of their minority, they are a minority.

Mr. Galbraith's boat slips silently along the bright blue line of the horizon. His horn is still, and no one waves. No: the son of the Jews does. He waves until the sea is empty again. Then he launches wood. The mother continues to read. The father has gathered himself higher upon the rock. He is a pale hand, fingers down on the top of the glinting smooth stone. He holds on. He stares at the empty ocean. When a low fishing ketch passes, and when his son waves and jumps at the beach's edge, the father watches very carefully. When the boat is gone, and the boy is straining at a log three feet around, which he cannot move, the father shakes his head. He looks behind him, slipping on his perch as he does, to see his wife, her book on her lap, watching him. She nods. He waves with his hand held low. She smiles down at her book, and he lets his arms and legs go so that he slides into the shape of stranded seaweed or starfish.

It is night, and the Galbraiths entertain. Three long cars are in their driveway. Their screened windows are bright with electricity and laughter and talk. The house of the Jews is dark once more. Sometimes the smear of candlelight slides onto a window. A buoy grunts. It is the second night of the Jews' vacation. It is the customary night, during New England vacations, for one or more members of a family to lie awake with the pain of sunburn.

But who can tell how it goes with these Jews? They are private people, and no one says why, if sundown is past and the Sabbath over, they persist in avoiding light.

On Sunday morning, the bells from little towns ring over the cold clear ocean air. Cars travel on the winding road. Some of them stop at the high-school baseball field—a foot-fogged diamond and six rows of salt-scoured bleachers—and some go all the way into the large town where there is a church, and a restaurant, a twenty-four-hour A&P, and a store that sells the Portland papers. The Galbraiths drive away in the Volvo, and the Jews walk down to the beach. The mother's neck has been burned by the sun, and the child is freckled and taking on the red-brown tone of ripe peaches. The father's nose is bright, as is his forehead. He wears a long-sleeved shirt and carries the pack basket in his hand. At the beach, the father and mother sit back near the raw logs deposited by winter storms. The boy walks down to the edge of the beach and then away, to where the rocks are larger and lead to cliffs and tide pools. He climbs until he is small over the ocean. The father and mother watch the child. The child lifts rocks over his head with both hands and hurls them down.

The interlopers arrive by sea, in a short high-hulled fiberglass boat with a large loud motor in the back. When they switch the engine off, crows and sea birds continue to call. The sound of the sea returns. The boy on the high rocks watches the boat wallow in the tide that now comes in. The mother puts her book down. The father looks at her hands. The hands clasp each other. The voices of the people in the boat blow toward the shore and

grow louder as the boat drifts close very quickly. There
is a woman in a white bikini. She has large breasts and
a roll of tight tanned fat beneath her navel. Her short black
hair moves softly. The man is of average height but with a
very broad rounded chest, thick soft arms, and large
stomach. He wears a pair of tight black trunks that com-
press a ring of dark flesh on each thigh. He jumps from the
boat and pulls it onto the beach and up, away from the
weight of the tides. As he looks at the parents, he smiles
and raises a hand. Then he and the woman carry canvas
bags ashore, to the other end of the beach. The child of the
Jews watches with his nose aimed at the newcomers, as if
he smells their spoor.

The man and woman walk past the Jews, behind them,
toward the end of the beach where the child is. The child
climbs above them as they walk beneath the cliffs to the
sandy places. The man delicately walks in a thin clear
stream and bends frequently, plucking mussels, which he
places in a pot the woman holds. Her swimsuit is thin
and her nipples show. In the sun, her body gleams as if she
has oiled it. The mother touches her T-shirt. The father
is holding the mother's book, turning pages.

Over a folding stove the man cooks mussels in the aluminum pot. The woman bends at the edge of the sea to
lift a bottle of white wine from the rocks that have
weighted it down against the tide. The man and woman
open the wine and sit on a tartan plaid blanket and eat
from the pot, drinking in turn. The Jews eat sandwiches
the father hands around from the pack basket. They
drink from paper cups that are filled from a thermos.

The boy carries his sandwich to the sea and, not far from the boat at which the tide now slowly beats, he throws his bread into the ocean. No sea birds dive to feed, and the bread turns transparent and sinks. The father calls softly to him, but perhaps the child doesn't hear. The father looks at the woman in the bikini and doesn't call again.

The woman lies face up on the blanket with her eyes closed. Her breasts settle against her. The man pulls at the hawser of the boat, then stops and calls the boy, who looks toward his parents, then approaches. Together, they pull the boat back from the tide. The mother has tied her T-shirt below her breasts with a large drooping knot. The father has rolled up his trousers and sleeves. The man and the child of the Jews are far off, to the left, standing on rounded rocks nearly surrounded by sea, casting with short rods the man has taken from his boat. The woman whose body gleams has risen on one elbow to watch them. The father looks at her back and buttocks. The mother does not. She is considering the long white boat that steadily approaches from the direction of the harbor. She points and murmurs and the father shrugs.

But the father looks too now as Mr. Galbraith rows his dinghy in while his pilot holds the forty-footer steady offshore and Mrs. Galbraith, aboard the boat, waves to the son of the Jews, who waves back. The man in the black swimsuit slowly walks through the surf to meet Mr. Galbraith. The woman in the bikini sits up, and the fold of fat gathers above the cloth of her suit. Her fingernails drift over her thighs, barely touching. The father watches the fingers. And the mother says, "You pig." The father stands and walks toward Mr. Galbraith and the man. "You pig," the mother says.

"Private beach," Mr. Galbraith is saying courteously to the man. Mr. Galbraith wears white deck shoes and light white trousers, a white long-sleeved shirt. His hands are in his pockets and he smiles as he speaks. His head and neck don't move. The woman in the bikini is standing, and her hands rest on her buttocks. The father stands between her and the two men. He turns to her and nods, then smiles, and she smiles back. Mr. Galbraith gestures at the cove, the field beyond it, and the two houses, one on each side of the one-lane road. "All a private compound," he is saying. The man holds his fishing rod and listens. Then, in a deep voice, he speaks of mussels and the afternoon and says, "We thought just for lunch."

"I prefer not to make that sort of exception," Mr. Galbraith tells him.

The woman in the bikini walks closer, and the father, as if he senses her, steps backward a few paces. With difficulty, as if himself in the heavy ebb of a tide, he turns on clumsy feet and is looking again at the woman in the bikini and talking to her, running his hands along his shirt and belt as if to clean them. His body is curved to suggest he is much taller than she, which he is not, and must stoop to better address her. Mr. Galbraith, behind them, says to the man, "Very soon, please. I prefer it that way, and I hope you understand." The father generates, for anyone to see, his urge to close with the woman, to grapple or caress. He nearly moves in place with energy. The woman holds her hands against the little rise of sun-tanned fat above her pelvis and chats, and the father replies.

As Mr. Galbraith turns toward his dinghy, as the father curves toward the woman, as the man watches Mr. Galbraith walk away, the mother screams and everyone looks to her and then to where she points. She screams again. The tide is higher now, and, to be sure, it has encircled the rock on which the child was fishing with the man. But is there actual danger? The child still stands on the rock, holding onto the rod that is connected by a slack line to the sea. The water is around the rock, but the child isn't frightened. Or is he? For his mother screams again, then again, and the child begins to cry. Mr. Galbraith's boat is afloat, and he climbs in and starts to row for the rock. He hasn't the necessary clearance for his oars, which strike bottom. The father says to the woman in the bikini, "Pardon me, please," and he runs along the beach until he is in the water to his ankles, slowed but still moving. The mother moves toward the rock, past the woman in the bikini, who catches her arm and says, "Let him do it." The man in the black bathing suit walks, hops, in the water, which is up to his thighs, and soon he is standing at the rock. He opens his arms and the child without pause leaps into them. The father, in water to his knees and fighting its pull, stands still. Then the father walks back up the beach.

The mother thanks the man. The man waves, then stoops to gather equipment to take to the boat. The woman sits in the boat, waiting. The Jews go up the trail toward the house.

. . .

It is almost dark. The lights are on at the Galbraiths. The windows of the house of the Jews are filled with reflected pinks of sunset. The child, outside in the gravel drive, eats a chocolate cupcake and moves his small green plastic soldiers into enfilades and bunkers arranged in the blue-white stones. The mother is very possibly naked on a bed upstairs, her long legs and short torso chilled in the air of dusk, which comes through a wide screened window facing the meadow and the pink and orange sea. The father probably sits, naked also, at the edge of the bed. Their child's voice from the driveway at the side of the house calls, "Okay, get ready now. You men hold your fire until I give you the signal. And no backtalk."

The mother opens her legs, in all probability, and says, "Well, bigshot?"

Or she says something else, her thighs close together in white denim shorts.

Or, in the kitchen, over coffee, her T-shirt pulled down again, her hands around the wide mug, she says nothing.

But who can tell? And who can speak of it? Especially now, with the sun down, the child inside, the windows dark. It is no Sabbath for the Jews, and yet these Jews are in darkness and the house yields nothing. The Galbraiths' windows throw their light upon the trimmed side lawn and the electric fence that separates yard from pasture where the dark shapes slowly drift.

S U N D A Y ,

L A T E

Sometimes they don't talk. Then there's the sigh of a beer can opening, and the wind, the gulls over Little Machias Bay. Jackson doesn't like it quiet too long. He'll say something like, "Anybody hear about Mac Stocking and old Meg over in Perry? Say, he got drunk Friday. He bounced so hard on the girl with that big belly of his, he put her into Eastport Hospital with her swivel loose." Then they'll laugh like dogs panting. Archibald Wesley's a serious man. He'll say, "There hasn't been haddock into Campobello three days running, you know. Men off'n the boats taken to saying the sea's died."

The North Cutler Volunteer Fire Department meets

after dinner every Wednesday night. They touch the siren off to test it and they write out their report according to State of Maine regulations. Then they open the beer and sit. The short-wave radio-scanner has six red lights that ripple one after the other, left to right. When they all go out, they start to ripple again. When someone broadcasts, the light above the radio band stays on, winking. Sometimes the voice from someone else's district is calm. Sometimes it shouts about people dying and buildings blowing in. The men look up.

You hear things in a firehouse. Sid's the youngest at forty. Lilian and Sid live fine. They've been married fifteen years. She's learning to be a poet. Wednesday nights, when Sid sits in the fire truck garage in North Cutler and listens to seven old men talk about fishing and federal welfare payments and how the owners closed off half the sardine cannery at Bucks Harbor Bay, Lilian goes to her seminar at the university in Machias and listens to some schoolteachers and poets do their talking. Lilian's younger than Sid is, and smarter. They went to school together. In a way, she still goes. She's always trying to learn. Now she wants to learn to be a poet. Sid tells her, "Just *be* one." She smiles.

Sid hears things. From Jackson, who sets out lobster traps. From Archibald, who sometimes works for Sid on contracting jobs. Archibald and Jackson do most of the talking. But the others talk too, and so does Sid. Whitney Cooper and his hog wrassle bobbed in and out of the smoking and swallowing and just sitting still for some time.

Whitney got up early, the way he always does. He's eighty-seven and he's tall. He looks like a strong man. Maybe he is, but he can't sleep so well anymore. He eats a package of Fritos for breakfast because he wants the salt. Living in that house over Little Machias Bay, at the end of a dirt road with the nearest neighbors there only in the summertime, he hasn't got any connection with the world except for his Bangor paper, which gets mailed in, and his big color television. His daughter visits now and then, and she takes him out to dinner a couple of times a year, and sometimes Wesley or one of the others will come and sit. But mostly Whitney's alone. You eat bad food when you're alone. So he had his breakfast, and he probably looked long and hungry at his bottle of Old Mr. Boston Rock and Rye with the colored fruit inside like something in a doctor's office in a jar. Then he went out to his Chalmers, which everyone is jealous of. It's a 1935 tractor big as an elephant and it runs better than his 1950 Dodge. His shed is stocked with spare parts and he re-builds the tractor when it breaks. He tends a garden not much bigger than a small front yard. That's what he was doing in late April, with the fog still heavy on the ground and everything cold. He was starting to get his garden in, dressed in his black serge pants held up by wide green suspenders, wearing the raggedy seaman's shirt and the hat he wore when he worked on the Governor's Friend-ship sloop in 1928 or '29.

The hippie—that's what Whitney called him—came down over Charlie Epping's meadow with that long downhill stride which is close to a run. You use it when you're too tired to keep your pace in check. Whitney said he looked old-fashioned, which is kind of funny for an eighty-seven-year-old man to say about someone in his thirties. But Sid supposed they hadn't been showing that kind of costume on TV for years. The hippie wore a bandanna around his long hair like a sweatband, and fringed trousers with wide bottoms, and no shirt, just a striped cotton vest that was open down the front. His boots were worn down at the backs and one sole was starting to flap. Archibald said that Whitney said the hippie's backpack looked heavy enough to sink a dinghy. He was tall and very thin, no fat anywhere, plenty of muscle. He stank of dried sweat. His teeth were yellow. His face was sunburned dark red. His nose was a big curving beak. With all that long hair and the sweatband and that kind of a nose on him, Archibald said, Whitney began thinking of him as the Indian. "Turned out to be a big-city Jew," Jackson said. Jackson's always worried about the Jews.

Sid remembers when it started, the Wednesday after the Indian turned up at Whitney's place. Sid told Lilian about it, and she said, "These days, you don't expect to see grown men walking around like that. Is he a writer?"

Sid said, "Nobody mentioned any writing. You want me to find out?"

Lilian said, "Not unless it comes up."

"They must have plenty of writers to spare in the seminar, Lil. Do you need another one?"

She just smiled.

Well, Whitney can be plenty deaf when he needs to be, so he just steered the Chalmers down another of his little rows, puffing up clouds of Holiday tobacco from the corncob between his false teeth, pretending he hadn't noticed the Indian stop, pretending he didn't hear him call. Someone said Whitney must have wondered whether he was off the Indian Township reservation near Peter Dana Point, but Sid didn't think so. Whitney's first wife had been part Indian, and Whitney'd know.

After a time, Whitney turned the tractor back and the

Indian was still there. Whitney put the Chalmers into neutral and let it idle. He sat over the big engine and watched what had to be the last hippie in America, standing there years after the breed had gone extinct, talking into motor noises with no hope of Whitney admitting he heard a sound. Whitney didn't like to be bothered unless he was drunk on Rock and Rye. And then he liked to choose who did the bothering.

So it was surprising that he reached over and turned the engine off and climbed down with that slow stinginess in the muscle that old men use whether they're going up the stairs or striking a match. Archibald said it was because Whitney was lonely. Maybe. Jackson said Whitney wanted someone to drink with. Nobody asked for Sid's opinion. He didn't try to form one. A week later, Lilian said it was because the Indian had a compelling personality. Sid didn't ask her how she knew.

They ended up in Whitney's house. The Indian bathed in Whitney's tub and put on the same wood smoke-smelling clothes, not talking much. Whitney didn't talk much, either. It was Saturday, so Whitney put his beans on for supper and after a while they watched the quiz programs on the Portland station. That night they ate the beans and some bread the Indian had bought fresh in Machias. They drank some of Whitney's Rock and Rye and looked at Whitney's favorite program, *The Lawrence Welk Show*. The Cutler Baptist Reunion was a month away. Whitney must have been thinking about it, but he wouldn't have mentioned it yet to a stranger. The Indian slept that night in Whitney's shed. And he stayed on.

Lilian wrote some poems about the squat white church at the corner above Whitney's house. Archibald Wesley says it's true, though he might lie about it to make you listen. The story is that Charlie Epping used to keep cattle in the pasture there. One August a couple of the heifers broke out and started off through Whitney's yard, then up the hill through the blueberry bushes and into the cemetery behind the church. Whitney was mad as hell when they ate the last of his peas. He took down his German 12-gauge and chased them. He was young then, in his sixties, and he got close behind them. He didn't know what to do with the gun, but he was determined he'd do something. What he did, finally, was fire off a barrel into the air, probably to frighten Charlie Epping. Charlie didn't even hear the shot. He was out in North Cutler at the laundromat, where he was custodian a couple of afternoons a week. But the charge sure frightened the cattle. They began to run. One of them ran over Whitney's son's grave. The earth was damp and soft, the top of the wood coffin was rotted through, and the hoof went straight down and jammed there. The leg snapped like a bough. The heifer began to bellow when Whitney came up. He hadn't stopped running before he put that shotgun up and blew the heifer's brains out all over his son's headstone. "All's I could see was the dumb bastard's foot in my boy's moldering face," is what Archibald said that Whitney said.

That's the story, and Lilian made a poem out of it. The people in her seminar liked it, she said. Along with the other one about the Cutler Baptist Church, about the time some old man ran away from his son and daughter and hid there upstairs for a couple of weeks. He lived with a camp stove and flashlights. People seeing the glow thought it was ghosts. The church had been abandoned after the congregation began to die off. A new church went up in Marshfield, and except for the Reunion no one ever went inside the old one. Thieves did break in a winter ago and stole the woodstove.

So when Lilian drove out to the old church about two weeks after the Indian came, Sid thought she was working on another poem. He had a job in Roque Bluffs, building a big summer house for some people from New York. He'd go early and come home late. They were offering a bonus if he could get it done in time for them to spend August there. He didn't think he could do it, do it right, but he was working at it. He stayed after his crew quit at four in the afternoon and worked as well as he could on his own. Lilian and Sid were taking separate meals because of that. He'd drag home after dark to sit with her for an hour or so before falling asleep. She understood him but she didn't like it. Not because she didn't want him to work the best he could, but because he was doing it for some rich people's bonus.

"Donkeys chase carrots," she said.

"That make me an ass?"

"Since when do you make puns?"

"Just in self-defense, Lil."

"And since when do you need to defend yourself from me?"

"Well, do I?"

"You tell me," she said.

"If I can raise my tired hands high enough to grab hold of you, then I will."

She said, "Oh, I think you can." And she was right.

He skipped a week at the firehouse because of the job. The following Wednesday, once they were sitting and the siren had blown, Jackson said to Sid, "What about this Indian of Whitney Cooper's?"

"I guess you'll have to tell me, Jackson. All I know's that he's still sleeping down there. He works in the garden with Whitney, I understand."

Jackson's round shiny face didn't give Sid any expression. He just said in that soft voice of his, "Oh. I thought maybe Lilian would've found something out."

Sid opened a beer and drank some. All he could think of to say was "No." He drank some more.

Jackson said, "Uh-huh." No one said anything for a while. Then Archibald started talking about a St. Regis pulpwood truck that had jackknifed near Cathance Lake. Sid drank and listened.

He left early but not too early to talk about when he had gone. Lilian had just come in from the seminar in Machias. She was making coffee and smiling, talking about a poem she'd read to the class, telling Sid what the people in the class had said. On seminar nights she left the electric lights off and they used the two kerosene lanterns in brackets on the wall above the table. Everything looked brown and yellow in the kitchen. They drank coffee and listened to the insects and the wind. She said a line of her poem the class liked, and he told her it was beautiful.

After a time they were silent. Then the silence went on. She watched him. She knows him. She said, "I gave Whitney Cooper's hippie Indian a lift the other day."

"Did you?"

"Just into Machias. He was hitching on Route 1. He wanted to buy that anadama bread they bake at Mackenzie's. I drove him back after I did my shopping."

"Good," Sid said. "What's he like?"

"His name is Barry Roth. He doesn't talk very much.

I think maybe that's why Whitney likes him—he listens, he's very quiet. Like you."

"Gonna get me a red bandanna sweatband to wear?"

"No, he *is*. He's quiet."

"Is he a writer like you thought?"

"He says he's a student. I guess if I'm not too old to be a student, he isn't either." She said, "He's younger than I am. Than we are."

"Where does he go to school?"

"He worked for half a year in California someplace, I forget, so he could afford to take this trip. He's taking this sort of *trip*, hitching and walking, buses, that kind of thing, camping out. He's just traveling now. But he studied at the University of California. He studied Oriental religions."

"And what does he do for a living?"

Her wide eyes and smile, her eagerness. That's what he was thinking about now. The face of a kid who's found a friend. Or something like that. She said, "Oh, I think he just wanders, hon. That's all. Isn't it strange?"

Sid told them what he knew at the next Wednesday night, like he'd set Lilian onto the Indian to learn what she could for the sake of their gossiping. Everybody nodded. They accepted what he could offer in the way of dignity. Then they went on to what they had learned. Which was plenty, since the Cutler Reunion was just a week away. It seems that several nights running Whitney had been all of a sudden called on by some of the men. They'd sat and talked with him and the Indian. They'd looked around. They reported what they knew or had decided was fair enough to make up. Speculation, maybe. But it surely sounded right, given Whitney's past, which was older than anyone there and somehow common property.

Whitney and the Indian had started into drinking the old Rock and Rye pretty regularly. It didn't take Whitney all that long to get himself easy enough with the Indian to start in drunken storytelling. Sometimes he'd wear his white seaman's belt and white shoes and his dress-white oceangoing cap. He would sit in his chair in front of the TV, shooting sparks out of his pipe, laughing loud sometimes, sometimes not talking at all, staring through the detectives and pink women, with the Indian in his fringed pants and vest on the sofa opposite.

This is what Sid thinks now. Something like this:

"Did I tell you once I was sexton at that gawdam church up there?" His long freckled hands waving at the hill above them. "Yes, I was. Georgie wanted me to do it. I rang their bell and mowed their lawn. They could have got a *goat*, but I did it. Every gawdam Sunday we would drive the car up the hill and turn around and park it pointing downhill on the lawn I mowed for them. I wanted to be ready for the getaway, you see."

The Indian would say, "That's right. I'm like that too."

"Yes, you are," Whitney would say. "And you're right to do it." But he wasn't listening. He'd gotten drunk so he could hurry into saying, "One Sunday Georgie and me—this was five years ago—we were driving up there. You look tomorrow and count up three telephone poles from this one and you'll see the road shoulder where it happened. Georgie was driving because she didn't trust my eyes. They were better'n hers, but you try telling *her* that. She was driving and she let go the wheel and folded over like a sack." Whitney would be swallowing his Rock and Rye, the tears would be running, his pipe would be out. "We were going slow and the car dipped down into the shoulder and stopped. I said 'Georgie!' like I was waking her, but there wasn't any waking her. No, sir. I knew she was sick and it was bad. Ran down the hill like a billygoat to get to my phone. I've always been on the telephone line. I called Dr. Morgan over in North Cutler. You know how gawdam long it takes a vehicle to get from North Cutler over here to Cutler? Couldn't be thirteen miles, but it's the gawdam curves in the road. He got here in time to tell me Georgie was dead. That's what he did."

The Indian would say, "I believe in the soul, Whitney. Do you? The immortal soul? So it's like she isn't all dead. I mean, she's *dead*, but not disappeared from your life. Like she's everyplace here. Or am I just—" The Indian would wave away his words from the air around him. After a few seconds, he would say, "Her picture's beautiful."

Whitney would snort his phlegm and light his pipe and shower sparks again. "Yes, it is. I married my first wife, Eleanor, because her mother all but put a cannon to my head. But we were all right. We were together twenty-five years. Then I was alone and then Georgie— I courted her in school, did I tell you that? Yes, sir. We weren't strangers. And when we got married, that was fine. And we were together fourteen years and I been alone five more." Then his eyes would squint and he would say politely, "I believe in being dead. I don't traffic with souls."

The Indian would say, "They're impractical. You end

up wasting all that loneliness. Like they don't seem dead, and they aren't around when you need them, either. If they're souls. Fair enough," he'd say. "But I keep hoping."

"You'll grow out of that," Whitney would say. "It's tiring. I haven't enjoyed a day for five years. I don't expect to. And I don't want another of these gawdam winters here, either. Don't expect to be here at the end of this one coming."

"You should stay, Whitney," the Indian would say. "You're a beautiful man. You stay here."

"Don't know as I'm beautiful," Whitney would say, "but I once used to be able to convince some of the ladies I was." He would sip his Rock and Rye and nod his head. "Yes, sir, I was forced sometimes to spread my manly energies thin, as you might say."

The Indian would make a circle in the air with his hand, directing them back to a starting point. "So why doesn't the minister understand about you and Georgie when you tell him? I mean about how you feel. Don't you tell him what it's like for you?"

"Tell him as little as I can when he catches me sitting still, the piss-ant. He's too old to think straight and too bent under all his gawdam righteousness to understand how a man can keep his anger on."

"Why do you want to be angry?" the Indian would say.

And Whitney would shift his thin long legs in the padded chair and wave a pointing finger, saying, "Don't you be too quick to advise me about anger, now. I've got cause. You're young, you're starting out, aren't you? Shit 'n gawdam there, Barry, I'm telling you what I *know*."

The Indian would sit perfectly still, then refold his

hands. After a silence he would say, "I've got a wife in California, Whitney, and she's got our daughter, and they both live in a bungalow in the north with a little man who makes his bread selling drugs. He sells a pop to a playground kid if he can do it—he sells speed to *dogs*, for chrissakes. He'd sell anything, anytime. I think he's selling my wife."

And Whitney would blunder on into it, saying, "There you are, then. You should know. What kind of pop is that you're talking about?"

The Indian would slowly shake his head. He'd say, "No. We can't just be angry. We have to *try* not being angry. We have to go *with* it." He would shake his head. "We—"

But Whitney would be beyond him, saying, "So every year that awful gawdam man brings his half-dead congregation back here for his gawdam hog wrassle. They sing their songs and do their little whispery prayers and pass the hat, hoping they can raise money to put a better roof on a church nobody wants to use. I guess they will, too, one of these days. If they don't all die out first. I'm the oldest one and they want me back in there with them. I don't know why, but I surely won't do it. No, sir. I told him a couple of years back. I won't go in there praying anymore. I did it and Georgie did it and the gawdam Lord in there took my first wife away and then He took my son away and then He took Georgie and He sentenced me to keep on living. No."

The Indian would be drinking his Rock and Rye. He would nod, and his head would stay down. His chin would be against his chest. He would put the drink back down on the floor again, his fingers tight against his pants.

"You know what I told him last year when he come

scratching?" Whitney would say. "I told him, 'Down here, we dance around a totem pole.' Gawdam if it isn't a fine idea."

At home that night, in the light of the kerosene lamps, Lilian told Sid about the seminar. One of the students had read a batch of little Japanesey poems aloud. Sid reported on what he'd heard, the Indian and Whitney's feelings about the Reunion. Lilian said, "I know," watching him.

Sid nodded and drank coffee.

"Barry came to the seminar," she said, rubbing her fingers on her notebook. "I guess he wanted someone new to talk to."

"How did he get there?"

"Oh, well, I was driving in and I saw him walking on the shoulder, so I gave him a lift. That was all right, wasn't it?"

"Sounds all right to me," Sid said.

She nodded. She smiled. She stopped smiling. "He did used to be married," she said. "He really still *is* married. His wife left him for this horrible-sounding man—I think she's a drug addict. She sounds horrible too."

"I don't wonder he'd walk to the opposite coast," Sid offered. It was the best he could do.

Lilian nodded, and Sid got up to pour them more coffee.

"It's amazing what a sorrowful past will do for a man," Sid said once he was sitting again.

"You mean teach him things?"

"I guess that, too."

He's sitting now with his fingers sliding over the corrugated stampings on the running board of the fire truck.

The red lights on the scanner are rippling. Sometimes voices cut in and a light blinks. The doors are open. No one's there now. He keeps looking at a beer can on the cement floor. He stands and starts to sweep. He gives it up and sits down again. He tries to see Lilian in her car with the Indian. He can't figure what she'd say. He keeps seeing her as shy. He closes his eyes so he doesn't have to see her face. The noise of the wind going past the open windows of the car. The smell of the Indian's cigarette. The smell of rotten lobster bait and tide flats. Maybe the smell of her perfume. The smell of the Indian's smoky clothes. Him saying something about someplace in California and did she ever pass through there. Her saying no, she'd been to Boston and New York a couple of times and once to Missouri when Sid was in the service.

He tries to move the Indian across the front seat closer to her but he can't. He tries seeing the car all of a sudden parked. Lilian moving over to the Indian in the still car on a dark road. He can't do that and his fingers bounce on the fire engine's running board. He makes everything darker and listens to clothes pulling in the parked car. He listens to her sigh and he thinks of soft skin and hard skin and he has to stop.

If it isn't flesh, what is it? Sid keeps thinking that whatever it is, it's hers. That is the part hurts the most. That he owes her that. Whatever it is. He's never owed her anything outside their house before. Except maybe the poetry classes. Maybe this is part of the classes. Like Whitney ringing the Cutler church bell and cutting the grass. He owed his wife. But at least it was something Whitney could *do*. This is something Sid is only allowed to listen to. And in the dark. It's hard being ignorant. Sid is learning that.

Then it was Sunday. He was working in the early morning on the Roque Bluffs beach house. There was little enough framing left for him to finish in a day. That meant he could free someone to start laying in the plywood subroof on Monday. The tide was coming in fast. It was over the rocks and nearly up to the driftwood in front of the tall grass. There was fog in the cove. Everything smelled of it. Sid heard the bells from the buoys at Roque Island and Englishman Island and Great Spruce Island in Chandler Bay. They were tinny and flat in the fog. He heard the deeper bells from the church in Kennebec and then maybe the long toll from the Cutler Baptist Church. It was Reunion Day.

Then he heard the siren go off. It was theirs, the deep hoarse sound. Then the Roque Bluffs and Kennebec sirens started. All the wailing smothered out the bells. He dropped his hammer and ran to the truck. He had to drive the very slow road up the point back to Route 1, then northeast until 191 cut in at East Machias. Then he had to go out along the Bucks Harbor Bay point to Cutler. It took too much time. He didn't drive safely. He had a feeling what it was.

Going past Cutler he didn't see the smoke he expected, but he hurried. By the time he made it to North Cutler, both fire trucks were gone. On the blackboard near the scanner it said CUTLER CHURCH. He ran back to the truck, backed around, headed out again on dirt roads that weren't much more than cowpath. He figured Whitney would set a fire right and there wasn't time for polite driving. Sid was half an hour late already.

The back of the truck was almost empty and it swayed and bucked on the roads. Once he hit a whanging great shot on a rock in the road and he looked in the mirror to see if oil was spraying, but he kept going. He skidded around the turn at the top of the hill above the church. The tanker was parked on a little rise, to give more pressure to the water going down into the pumper truck. But the trucks were just parked there, their lights swinging around. No hoses ran between them. Archibald and Jackson and the rest stood in their black slickers and watched. Sid saw Lilian's car, then Sid saw Lilian. She was in front of the church. Around her in a half circle were the twenty or so old people in bright colors. The minister stood with them, talking. Everyone was watching Whitney. He had a bottle in his hand. The Indian held him straight. Sid could tell Whitney was screeching up at the church.

The Kennebec company came in behind Sid and he got out and waved them down. He told them to go back home, it was a false alarm. Grunwald from Kennebec was fat, and he was meaner than he usually managed to be. He said Archibald had put out a false-alarm report on the radio to anyone in the area who might respond, including Kennebec and Roque Bluffs. Grunwald said he and his company had come on in anyway because they wanted to see what kind of a bastard son of a bitch would ruin a Sunday morning and scare everyone shitless just to have some fun. Sid told him he didn't think there was any fun in it, but Grunwald got back in his truck and drove down. He made sure his siren and hooter and lights were on, just in case somebody failed to understand it was serious business once a fire engine rolled. Sid got back into the truck and he stayed there, watching. He didn't want to go down the hill.

He saw Lilian move away from the congregation and the little cluster of local people who'd come to help or watch. She went closer to the Indian and Whitney. Sid couldn't hear anything except the motor and some shouts. He listened, though. Sitting there now, in the fire department garage, he's still listening. To the Indian saying, "Now it's all over, Whitney. Let's go home and talk," his arm around Whitney's neck like Whitney was his child.

To Whitney saying, "Isn't over until I'm dead, gawdammit. Gawdam pious hog wrassle! I said we do our dancing round a totem pole down here and I meant it. Tell 'em, Barry. Tell 'em what I'm owed." Sid saw Whitney slipping as the Indian tried to hug him with both bare arms, heard Whitney shout, "Don't get clutchy with me, dammit! Who's in charge of putting me in jail? I'm ready for 'em."

Lilian moving closer. Sid couldn't tell who she wanted to touch, but her hand was cocked. Then she stood behind the Indian. She didn't let her hand move. Sid could feel its muscle tense, then yield. She turned around and looked at the congregation. Her lips moved but of course Sid didn't hear what she said. He's known her nearly twenty years. He's sitting here in the garage, thinking about it. He still can't make up what she might have said. She's the one he knows the best and he can piece together what a stranger might say, but not his wife. He wonders if she knows that.

After a while the sheriff came past Sid with his lights going. The congregation watched. Whitney's married daughter came, and she and Whitney drove down to his house in the sheriff's car. People started to move, and then cars left, then the engines came up and passed Sid. Some of them waved. Jackson stared. In front of the church, the Indian talked to Lilian and she answered him. He nodded

his head and she nodded back. Then he walked down the
hill toward Whitney's house. She watched him walk.
Then she got into her car and drove up the hill. When
she saw the truck, she turned left, went past Sid a few
yards and parked. He walked over.

Lilian leaned her arm out the open window and put her
mouth down into the crook of her elbow. Sid stood there
and looked in. He said, "Old Whitney."

She said, "I came down when I heard the siren. I
thought it would be him. Barry said he was getting bad."
Her face looked older.

Sid said, "I guess it just got to him after all this time."

"What did?" she said. She looked at Sid and he felt
uncomfortable.

He waved his hand downhill, toward the church, or
Whitney's house, the bay. "I don't know," he said. "Just
everything, I guess."

She nodded into her arm.

He said, "I'll see you at home later on, all right?"

She raised her head and looked into the rearview mirror and said, "I'll be ho—what'd you say?"

"I said I'll see you there."

"At home?"

Sid nodded.

"All right," she said, "I'll see you at home."

After she left, Sid sat in the truck. Then he drove to
North Cutler. The men were stowing breathing tanks and
the respirator, and Jackson was pushing a rag over the
brasswork. The others were leaving. Jackson said, "Say,
wasn't your wife cut up over all of that?"

"She's a poet," Sid said. "She takes things hard."

"Well," Jackson said, "I guess."

Jackson began to whistle as he polished. He stroked the truck like that for a while, then put the chamois rag in a box against the wall and went home. Archibald came over and sat on the running board next to Sid. Archibald didn't say anything. Then he left too.

Sid is listening.

MY FATHER,
CONT.

If anything was growing just because it was March, it was
growing under cover like the rest of us. Snow still rode
the eaves and trembled in the skies, the banks of black-
grained ice stood three feet tall at the sides of the roads
and over all the lawns. But the calendar said spring, and
the local newspapers said spring, and even the TV shows
from New York, piped into Syracuse and Utica, then out
among the small winding roads and old hills to the brand-
new pastel trailers and the old gray clapboard farmhouses
—the farmers lived in the trailers; the city people, in
heralded perpetual retreat, lived in the farmers' abandoned

homes—said spring. What made it worse was that when all the official organs of the world's conspiracy for early spring made their announcements, the Solsville Cooperative Nursery School Book Sale made theirs. When that happened, I kept my mouth shut tight. I had read my *Hansel and Gretel,* and I knew what parents did with kids when there wasn't enough—and never mind *what*—to go around.

My father was a doctor and an ex-convict. That's how he used to describe himself to people he had just met and had drunk a couple of George Dickel sour mash whiskeys with: "I'm a doctor of children and an outcast of the people. I sat out the war because I didn't believe in killing, and sometimes the care these troglodytes up here give their children is enough to drive me past Korea and my conscientious objection and into the pits of pure murder."

He had been divorced, and I had a couple of older half-sisters someplace in the Middle West. He had married a pretty young woman who wrote a children's book when she was twenty and who never wrote a word again unless it was on a sign announcing a nursery school book sale or a rummage to benefit the local members of the Future Farmers of America. I was their issue, and I knew what was coming since it was calendar spring but actual winter, and my mother had just told him he should go upstairs to his study, an extra bedroom really, and take down his old paperback duplicate books and this year give in, for God's sake, and donate them to the Solsville Nursery School Book Sale and be charitable for once.

"Listen, Edna," my father's voice said. It hummed on the floorboards upstairs in my room and poured up through the old-fashioned heating vents. It was Sunday and I was waiting for the Celtics' game and looking at the horrible illustrations in *Hansel and Gretel*. It's the story about the family with too little to eat. They kept taking the kids into the forest and leaving them there because there wasn't enough to go around. It's the saddest story about families. It's the one that says hunger comes first. "Listen, Edna," my father said, "I don't mind taking their calls at six in the morning, and I don't mind chugging out at midnight to an obscenely underequipped rural emergency ward. I'll treat their kids and wait three years for them to pay their bills. All right—"

"Hold it, Hank," my mother said. She was closer to my age than his, I always thought, and smaller, like me, and nearly as smart as he was, which I wasn't. She had also said, one night, when I could hear them, that if it wasn't for me, she'd be long gone from his bucolic infantilism. I didn't look it up because I didn't want to know. But I wasn't pleased with how things were going for us. My mother said, "You won't be giving your precious thirty-five-cent paperbacks that are fifteen, twenty years old to the same pasty-faced potato-fat kickers you cure, Dr. Schweitzer. They don't read, remember? You're giving books that will be sold by the nursery school so it can keep the profits and stay open another few months and take care of the children of some faculty members at a small and undistinguished state college who nevertheless are the only friends you've *got*. Remember?"

He didn't whine but he seemed to, nearly, when he said, "Honey, it doesn't *feel* right to give my books away like that."

There was a little silence, and then she said, very low, "They're my books too, aren't they?"

And then another little silence, and then he said, "I'll do it. Do that again, and I'll do it."

And then another little silence and a long silence.

I went back to *Hansel and Gretel*—the part where the father gives in and says, "Ah, but I shall regret the poor children."

Later on, my father thumped up and down the creaky wooden stairs of the old farmhouse—between the phone calls he always got on Sundays from patients who should have seen him on Friday or waited till Monday—and he carried some cartons of books out to the station wagon. I heard the doors slam as he loaded the old paperbacks into the car. I was watching a basketball game on TV because I had finished my schoolwork and needed something full of team spirit—Bob Cousy being given the ball because he was lighter than air and he glowed in the dark and he *deserved* the love he was getting. I didn't want to think any more because I didn't understand what I was thinking. I didn't want to read any more about those kids in the forest because I did understand what I was reading. And that's why my heart was poisoned like a witch's pancakes when my father said over drinks in the living room—I could hear him breaking their long silence, which was hard on all three of us—"Let's go up into the hills, in near Brookfield, and see if the deer are coming down yet."

I hoped that when my mother answered, "It's too early," my father would drop the idea. She pushed him: "It's too early for the deer to come down, Hank. What they want is corn stubble, and the fields are still covered with snow. And they sure don't want more snow. They can get plenty of that up where they are."

As soon as he started to answer, I could tell from the swollen sound of his voice that she had made a big mistake.

Cousy glided in from fifteen feet out, it felt like, for

a slow-motion shot that made me hold my ears and shake my head. The Celtics surrounded him and they all slapped each other's buttocks and nodded and walked around with each other. I thought, *Ah, but I shall regret the poor children.*

My father said, "Well, Our Lady of the Charitable Mysteries and Reliquary Book Sale, if it's too early for deer, then it's too early for books, on account of both depend on spring, which has to do with the pagan notion of the earth reborn, and the Christian's juvenility about his Lord. If the deer won't come down, being a medieval symbol, then the Christ is not arisen. And if *He* won't be bothered, then I surely don't have to commemorate a spring which hasn't come by carrying my private property down to Solsville to watch them give it away."

My mother said, "You never should have stayed away from the war. You were meant for it."

I turned Cousy off and went for my coat and boots. When they called me, I was ready. They were surprised.

It was getting colder, and the air smelled wet, like snow coming. My father drove slowly and sighed, as if he were relaxing. The back seat of the wagon was down, and I sat with my back against their seat, my legs on the floorboards pointing out the back window, my elbows propped on cartons of books. I listened to my parents breathe and thought about the father saying, *We are going into the forest to hew wood, and in the evening, when we are ready, we will come and fetch you.* Of course I was intelligent and enlightened and, according to my mother and father, I lived in a climate of reinforcement, so all I had to do was lean back in the darkness of the car and the darkness of the ending day and watch as we crossed Route 1 2 and drove up the rutted icy roads, past gray houses with dull yellow lights in the windows, past mobile homes with eighty-foot antennas, to see how too smoothly we slipped into the woods.

In the summer there, you'd mostly see the maples and ash and beech, what elms were left, and the evergreens filled the spaces between. But in the early autumn, as the leaves fell, there was a kind of dance. First the trees weren't bare, because they bloomed bird's nests, vacant and ragged. Then the wind took some of the nests, or you stopped noticing them, and there was a lot of emptiness around. Then it was winter, and the evergreens seemed to step forward, the annual bearers seemed to recede, and then what you saw was snow, the hard brown roads, the evergreens covered in white, and the scraggly wisps of deciduous trees waiting for spring so they could step back into full sight. It was a slow exciting dance, and I miss it, but I won't go back to watch.

My father smoked his pipe, the car filled with smoke, my mother sneezed, and he drove up steep roads, past all houses now, into darkness, the lights still off. The car shivered and slid on its heavy snow tires, but he pushed it up. My mother said, "I think we should go back, Hank. It's early for deer, it really is. We always do this. We always come looking too early."

The tires whined, but he kept the car moving. I drew my knees up on the floorboards beside me and leaned over the seat, looking forward now, sniffing in the pipe smoke, letting an elbow touch each parent's shoulder in the fragrance and darkness of our ride. I saw the branching-off of our snowy road; in the darkness, the snow seemed to glow with a light from underneath it, and then the secret light went out as my father turned the car lights on, and we were coasting downhill slightly, but pretty fast, at a fork.

I would have stopped. My mother said it very clearly, that she thought we ought to. He let the car slide left, and we went downhill farther, maybe fifty or sixty yards. The car slid hard, then stopped—as if cement had just that moment turned from fresh to ten years old around the wheels.

"Okay," my mother said, "we're stuck."

"No," my father said. He floored it in forward gear, then shifted to reverse, floored it again, then shifted forward, then into reverse, and the wheels whined, the motor roared, a cloud of snow and exhaust blew up behind us, and the car stayed where it was. "Maybe not," he said.

The heater was on full, and it was getting sweaty in there, and the smoke from his pipe seemed suddenly a little sweet. I thought of sweets, of poisoned pancakes, and I said, "Hey, Dad, are we really trapped here? Can we get home?"

My mother said, "Shh," but it was too late.

My father, who was tall and heavy, and whose hair was an unkind color, like a metal you might find in a factory or a hospital but never around the house, shouted, "Well, of *course* we're going to get home! For Christ's sake. Do I really have to answer that kind of question now? Of *course*, dammit. And we'll get home in the goddamned *car* is how we'll do it."

I didn't answer, and he said, "Right?"

"What, Daddy?"

"I said *right*?"

"About what, Daddy?"

"*Jesus!*" he said. He slammed the door closed when

he got out, and he walked through snow that looked sometimes to be up to his calves and sometimes his knees as he went to open the tailgate, pull out the folding army-surplus shovel, and bend behind the steady red shine of our tail lights to stoop and push, rise and heave—I can see that now, at any time, in a crowd or in my sleep, that steady red-tinted rise and fall of my father in the forest, hewing. My mother held to the forearm of my heavy jacket. But I moved away. I watched.

The shovel flashed red as it crossed in front of the light, and so did his hands, and so did his face as it dipped to rise. He was chopping us out, and once he looked in, panting, blowing, the sweat on his face a bloody wash in the tail lights' falsifying glow—he would have loved to see himself like that, and perhaps he was looking at his reflection in the glass—and he smiled at me and asked forgiveness with his grin, as he usually did. But then he got angry again, frustrated, and his head bobbed up and down again, his face was hidden, as he dug at all the snow in the Brookfield forest.

After a while my mother said, "I hope he doesn't have a heart attack."

I said, "Can I dig? Can I take a turn? That'll keep him from having a heart attack."

My mother said, "He is so determined to have a heart attack, neither one of us can do a thing to keep him from having his way. Your father's a baby."

I said—and I don't know why; it was no wisdom, it was only *talk*, and yet maybe it was my memory of the woodcutter's wife—I said, "Should you be saying things like that about your husband?"

My mother squealed. Her head retreated, like a turtle's. She opened her mouth wide, and I saw her tongue

quivering. The door boomed and my father hurled himself in behind the wheel, panting, heaving against his
clothes. My mother closed her mouth.

I said, "Don't have a heart attack, Daddy."

"Absolutely not," he said. He rocked the car forward,
then from forward to reverse, reverse to forward. But we
didn't move. The metal of the motor screamed, and he
stopped. He said, "One more shot at it." I thought of the
family who didn't have enough to go around. I thought
of wandering among the thick, self-reliant trunks of trees
which went so far up I couldn't see their tops. Making no
progress. Wandering in terror. Gagged by my own
tongue. My mouth freezing open, yes, the tongue iced to
the roof of the icy mouth. I thought of the snow turning
black, the tree trunks white, my body going from white to
black. My black tongue frozen in my mouth, my black
teeth biting at nothing. Black wind pouring in and out.
Everything black down past my tonsils to my teeth and
stomach and my bowels. Then I saw my eyes, and they
were black marbles. I thought of people knowing that I
was there forever and not mourning—but regretting it.

My father, leaning over the seat, interrupted me by
saying, "Give me the books."

"What?"

"The goddamned *books*, goddammit!"

My mother said, "Don't take it out on him, he's
frightened enough."

"I'm not frightened," I said.

"I'm not taking it out," my father said. He stopped
moving, then started again, this time talking in a higher
voice. I guess he thought what was higher was lighter as
well. He reached in past my arms and legs and hauled
things into the glow of the glove compartment light: "A

soupçon of Thomas Hardy, I think. Ah, just right: *Jude the Obscure*, famous family man. Never did get his degree, as I recall. Yes. And some *Dickens*! Come on, Chuck, let's have the old *Bleak House* there and—oh, my land, how generous, he's giving us *Tale of Two Cities* too. Now that's what I call *giving*—somebody needs books, you give *books*. Am I right? And Miss Brontë, I believe? So kind of you to hurl yourself into the effort." He chuckled like what a mad scientist is supposed to sound like, and I guess that was meant to reassure us. I passed a few more over to him, and he took them and went around to kneel behind the rear wheels. We heard him grunting even though the motor still chugged in a ragged neutral.

Without asking permission, I got out. I took the flashlight with me, but I kept it off. I stood with the whole world behind me, and maybe because the road sloped, it felt as if everything could tip upon us, pour down onto us, and sweep us farther along. The snow was glowing again since he'd turned the car lights out, the all-but-darkness of the forest seemed to make the snow burn brighter from within. My mother looked through her window at me. She smiled a kind of smile, and I did it back.

My father had finished wedging the paperbacks beneath the tires—his last hope for traction—and then he got in to put the car in gear and floor it. I stayed where I was, my hands cupped over my ears so that I wouldn't hear the engine scream this time. Jude and his babies and Ellen and Sydney Carton and Catherine Earnshaw and Heathcliff flew from beneath our wheels, were torn by the deep treads into tiny fragments and blown behind us and up into the air. They sailed there, half in darkness, then down into the brightness of the glowing snow, and then they were carried by the wind and were ridden away. They were gone by the time my mother and father, ponderous in their snow gear, came out. Bulky as they were, they were as prone to flight and disappearance as the tiny papers and their black invisible words.

A couple of chunks of the stronger covers lay in odd designs behind the wheels. I was looking at what was left, and thinking of the family where hunger was foremost, and where there simply wasn't enough to go around. My father, I saw at last, was looking at me. He was grinning.

He said, "Ain't I something?"

"We go looking for deer," my mother said, "delicate gentle little hungry deer, and look what we end up with. A dead car and"—pointing at my father, at the woods— "this."

I said, "You really messed up, Daddy. You got us lost in the woods and everything." He shrugged, then turned to shut off the motor, lock the car up. I watched him as he walked around the car, being certain. I said, "I guess we didn't get *that* messed up."

He came back and stood before me. He said, "You think I screwed things up for you?"

I was shivering by then. I turned the flashlight on and pointed it at his face. There was no body and there were no woods. There was my father's face, and the darkness.

He looked into me the way some people peer into rooms. He saw what I was seeing. Looking away from me, and down at his vanished body, then into me again, he said, "Do I look like a ghost to you? Are you really good and scared?"

I started to cry. I let go of all of it and cried very hard.

"I'll get you home, love," he whispered down onto the

top of my head as he hugged me. "I'll get you out of the woods and I'll get you into your house and before you know it, you'll be laughing. I can do that for you, love."

I felt my mother move in to hug us. She pulled at the flashlight and I let it go. I kept my eyes closed and felt the dark woods tilt upon us.

My father—who was not a woodcutter, and for whom the hungers did not consistently come first—said, "It's all right. I'm not a ghost. There aren't any ghosts."

And for some good time he was right.

WHAT

YOU MIGHT

AS WELL

CALL LOVE

Just like a curse, rain fell for two weeks, hissing on shingles and in nearly naked trees, and the river, dammed by brush and rotted elms, began to rise. Sun sometimes shone, and sometimes the rain held off an hour, but the ground was always spongy, and mud was on everything. The river wound around the hamlet, in some places close to backyards, in others separated from yards by hillocks and cabbage fields. It was a dark autumn, and always cold; the cabbage stank in the early mornings and late at night. And the water table rose in response to the rain and pushed through deep foundation stones and up through cracked cement cellar floors, pooled around furnaces and freezers and water heaters, triggered sump pumps which gargled out the water which ran back into the ground and reappeared inside, rising slowly, in the darkness of the cellars looking black.

On the second day of flooding, Ethan came home from school with the mimeo'd message about the outbreak of head lice in the elementary grades. Marge had come up from sweeping pooled water in the cellar and her black boots glistened as she read the notice and cross-examined Ethan about school, while, forcing his head down, she raked through the fine brown hair, seeking nits.

"What's a nit?" Ethan said.

"You're clean," she said. "A nit is the egg of a louse."

"Louse?"

"A louse is one lice. Lice are a lot of louses."

"What's a *person* who's a louse, then?"

"A nitwit. Please go up and change your clothes."

"Can I look at the flood?"

"There *isn't* any flood. There's water in the cellar and go upstairs and change your clothes. Please. Everything's fine."

"How come you were down there, then, Mom?"

"I was sweeping water into the sump. It collects some places, and doesn't go into the sump. If that happens, it doesn't get pumped out. See? Please go up?"

"But doesn't it come back *in*?"

Marge sat on the floor and took one boot off. "That is not a nine-year-old question," she said. "Up."

Ethan said, "It's a nitwit question." He gave her his grown-up smile, irony and all, ruffled her thick light hair, and went up. Marge took off her other boot and leaned

against the wall, stretching out her legs, to wait for Ben
to come home.

He came in a red-and-black woolen shirt that was darkening with rainwater, and wire-rimmed glasses that were
sheeted over, and thirty feet of black plastic pipe taped in
a big crooked circle. As Marge held the door, Ben backed
and sidled and swore—"Sell. We sell, and we move someplace where we can live on top of a hill and *nothing* runs
in"—and then he was inside their small kitchen, talking in
a low rant and forcing the pipe around the table to the
cellar door.

Marge said, "You got it."

"The pipe? You noticed, huh?"

"According to Ethan, who is correct, the water is
welling *up*."

"What?"

"That water's coming *up* from the ground."

"You noticed that too, huh?" Ben was down on the
cellar steps now, pulling the pipe after him and grunting.

In a far, partly lighted corner, water ran in black
smears down the wall stones and onto the cement floor.
In the center of the floor, a hole three feet deep, about
eighteen inches in diameter, received the runoff from the
walls and floor. Tied to various beam jacks and ancient
wooden posts, some with bark still on them, held in a
web of white sash cord, was the sump pump with its copper float; when water in the sump reached a certain level,
the float came up and the pump started. Water ran from
it through black plastic pipe such as Ben wrestled with,
and up through a broken storm window above their heads,
and out onto the ground beside the house. The motor
went on and off twice as they watched, and Ben cleared

his throat and sniffed as if the need for pumping, the sound of the little motor, the invasion of water, were making his sinuses pour.

He lugged the pipe around the furnace to the other side of the cellar. There water pooled deeper than anywhere else, in a declivity that didn't permit it to run to the sump. They looked at it, and as Ben began to swear Marge went upstairs and put her boots on.

Ben stood above the center of the pool which shimmered, bubbled slightly, in the light of a bulb on the ceiling. In the pool was a silted corroding pipe. He leaned the circle of black plastic pipe against the furnace, squatted in the water, almost sitting in it, and jammed a plastic joint into the pipe in the floor. "It fits!" he called. "I guessed, and I was right, and it *fits*! I'm telling you, Marge, I'm going to pipe the goddamn water right the hell out of this old well or whatever the hell it is, *directly* into the faithful sump and its obedient pump, chug chug master, and we are *home*! There will be *no* pooling of water in my house without written permission. The furnace will continue to roar, *all* the necessary machines will function, including us, and the home fires will burn. Marge?"

She stood a few feet away from him, and when he noticed her he smiled, and then they both were silent as he pushed the elbow joint deeper into the rusted socket. There was the sound of dripping, and of the pump cutting on and off, and then the louder yammer of the water pump forcing water upstairs from their well because the pressure to the faucets was low, and then, at the same time, the whir of the furnace fan. Then the machines completed their cycles and stopped, and there was only the sound of their breathing, of trickles and drips.

Ben cut the tape from the black plastic pipe and Marge

took one end to stretch it away from him. She wove it among lolly columns and beam supports to where it would empty into the sump. "Mere victory," Ben said. "Nothing great. Maybe a small cathedral's worth of vision and ability and strength. Thank you."

Marge, looking at the open end of the pipe, which still was dry, which carried nothing from the rusted drain into the sump, said, "It does flow up."

"Water doesn't flow up."

"It *wells* up. It seeps. It's like a spring, Ben, when the water table's high. It comes up around the pipe you put there. It just comes up."

"Jesus, Marge."

She walked back to where he stood at the elbow joint and, stooping, pointed. In the silt around the pipe into which he had shoved the white plastic joint, water was bubbling up, stirring mossy brown sediment. The pool of dark water widened. Ben took the big janitor's broom that leaned against the furnace and he began to sweep, long hard angry strokes, so that the pool ran over the lip of its margins and flowed along the inclines of the cellar, into the sump. He said, breathing hard, "It doesn't work."

"Nice try, though."

"I really thought it would work. I thought seventeen dollars' worth."

"It was a good idea," Marge said.

"I should have listened."

"Ethan figured it out."

"Yeah? He's nine and I'm only thirty-five."

"Ben has the advantage of years," she said.

He threw the broom into the pool, which was widening again, and said, "I don't really think it'll get into the furnace."

"No," she said, "it probably won't."

"We'll check on it."

They were walking up the narrow steps.

"There's an epidemic of head lice in school," Marge said.

"Ethan's okay?"

"So far. But it's really contagious."

"Son of a bitch!" Ben said.

Marge said, "I'd rather have locusts than lice."

"You're right," Ben said at the top of the stairs. "There's a better tone to locusts than lice."

"And it seems more suitable to floods, anyway," Marge said.

Ethan was waiting in the kitchen. "I thought you said there wasn't any flood, Mom."

She sat on the floor, thin, with long arms, looking like a child as she took her black boots off. She said, "There isn't."

"Didn't you and Dad just talk about one?"

"It's a flood for grown-ups," Ben said. "It isn't a flood for kids."

"Nitwit," Ethan said.

And Ben roared, "*What?*"

Marge said, "It's a joke, Ben. It's a joke Ethan and I were having. Ethan, why don't you go upstairs and change your clothes?"

"I just did. Remember?"

"Why don't you go upstairs and read *John Sevier, Pioneer Boy?*"

"I finished it last night. Mom, would you and Dad like some privacy? I can go upstairs and work on my carrier."

Marge told Ben, "It's an atomic supercarrier which is capable of holding a hundred and ten assorted fighters and long-range patrol planes, plus surface-to-air missiles. One inch to forty feet. Good-bye, Ethan. I love you."

They were sitting in the kitchen with whiskey and ice, and Ben was telling Marge about an issue of the pharmaceuticals firm's company magazine he was putting together, for which he was not only editor but photographer and writer. He said, "Substitute teaching may just be the worst work in the world, and *I* wouldn't do it. I don't blame you for hating it. I'm saying, for *me*, right now, even though I did worse work in New York, this one is an ugly boring stupid horrible job. I mean, I think I'm running out of sick leave from calling in with phony flus every other day."

"And you don't get paid enough," she said.

"Nope."

"And neither do I, when I do get work."

"Nope."

"And we're out seventeen bucks for plastic pipe."

"Thank you," he said, "for recollecting that. For diving deep into your memory to retrieve that data."

"Datum."

Ben said, "Do I need another drink or do you?"

"Why don't we both do that, and skip the fight we don't even feel like having, and discuss what to have for dinner."

"Let's go out for pizza," Ben said. "Ethan loves it."

"Because it'll cost more money."

"Which we haven't got."

"Almost. We almost haven't got it, you're right."

Wind threw rainwater, as if it were solid, at the back-door window, and Ben said, "Fucking rain."

Marge stood, poured more whiskey over fresh ice for them, pulled at the hem of her sweater, and remained standing as she said, "I would like us to consider having another child."

Ben said nothing, drank a large swallow, stared at her. He offered a smile, the sort you use in case a bearer of bad news might be joking, then he withdrew it. The pump went on and off, then on again, then off. "It always sounds like it's grinding something," Ben said.

Marge said, "I realize this isn't the best time to broach the subject. But it's not a complete surprise."

"No. I was just hoping I could evade it for a while. Maybe until the rain stops?"

"Well, the rain keeps making me think about babies. It's the *threat*. Do you know what I mean? What if something, I keep thinking, what if something happens."

"You mean to Ethan?"

Marge's eyes filled and instantly were red at the rims. She nodded.

"We won't *let* anything happen to him," Ben said, as if he were accused of neglect.

"We can't stop the lice," she said. "We can't stop the rain."

"We're *old*, Marge. Aren't we pretty old to be having kids?"

"We're poor, and it's a nuisance, taking care of a baby again. But a thirty-five-year-old woman can deliver a child safely, a normal child, without risking her health."

"Not without risk."

"Without risking that *much*."

"Is that true?"

She drank some whiskey. She said, "I can find out."

In a khaki slicker and rubber boots, wearing a tweed hat, Ben walked the river. Behind him, the cabbage fields went slightly uphill and then descended to their yard and the backyards of seven other small box-shaped hundred-and-fifty-year-old farmhouses that had rank-smelling cellars and sodden lintels and rotting beams. In the late summer, when the cabbages were young and small, aquamarine, not stinking, thousands of small white cabbage butterflies hovered in the field, invisible until one of them caught the sun and then drew attention to the others, and what had seemed to be hundreds of rows of blue-green vegetables set into rock-studded light brown soil suddenly would seem an ocean of little butterflies that surged around the houses and their small yards. Now the cabbages were bulbous and dark, part of the muddy field that, despite its slope, could not keep the water table from rising through stone toward a furnace's fuel jet.

Ben broke through a natural fence of brush, some red poisonous berries still glistening but most fruit gone, and the vegetation a tangle of blackthorn and exploded milkweed and powdering log, pulped fungus. He sank in down to his calves and had to work himself loose. His boots freed with slow-motion sucking sounds, and there was a released smell of gases from the rotted roots and weed. He went downhill the last few yards, a steep muddy incline leading to the river's edge—higher than it ever had been—where sinuous dying elms stood on both sides of the river, which roared like machines. Debris floated past, chunks of log, plastic milk bottles, a bran-

colored kitten, turning. The surface was like a skin, for
although it sped, there was an undercurrent, other water,
deeper, moving more quickly. The surface was Prussian
blue and silver, bright, dangerous-looking, like a reptile's
skin. The water below was muddy and poisoned by cess-
pools rising with the flood.

It was deeper than ever, and faster, high enough to
cover a tall man, swift enough to drown him as it had the
kitten. Ben threw a heavy rounded chalky rock into the
water. It made no ripple or splash, but disappeared.
Slowly, as if he balanced at great heights, Ben walked
along the river toward the red iron bridge at the south
end of town. He passed behind the homes of two widows,
and the only man he knew who was always glad—Henry
Quail, seventy, fat, smelling of chewing tobacco and
sweat and Irish whiskey. Because of his cleft palate, Henry
was hard to understand, and few people asked him to speak.
Henry patrolled the roads in his long green pickup truck,
answered fire alarms in his red reflecting vest and yellow
hardhat, helped repair tractors, collected his Social Secu-
rity, made large and undeclared sums for cutting the horns
off cattle, and was always bright-faced drunk.

In the large backyard of the second widow, water had
collected six inches deep at least. A pyramid of logs, waiting to be split—probably by Henry Quail—had fallen,
and some of the logs were submerged in the pool. Then
the field between the river and the hamlet climbed again,
steeply, and there was no cabbage; at first there were rows
of corn stubble which, as the snows melted, the deer might
come to crop at dusk, and then there was only tangled
brush and high weed as the land rose to close Ben in at
the river's turning.

The elms were bare above him, close together, soon

to die and fall. Some willow flourished there, the empty branches hanging like awful hair, suddenly shuddering as the wind picked up. The temperature was dropping as darkness fell, and a mist hung above the water, higher than a man could reach, thick and smelling of cabbage and silt and old plants. The fog looked yellow in the dusk light. The roar of the river grew as Ben went on and arrived at the dam.

At first it looked as if the silver-blue skin of the water had grown tumorous. Then he saw, just under the surface, tangled trees, woven vines, and bushes locked into one another, small logs and larger ones, pieces of siding, detergent boxes, green garbage, bones. All were holding the river high, though a million gallons flowed past him as Ben watched. He closed his eyes and opened them, lost the peculiar focus he'd found, and saw simply a silvery blue skin that writhed.

He went on to the bridge, from which children in summer fished and where Ben had stood to watch Ethan and some friends wade on the sun-heated slippery rocks. Now they would, as soon as a foot went into the water, be seized and beaten, pulled away, spinning, to surface half a mile downstream, under the railroad trestle, features erased by rocks and trees, bloody tubes of meat digested and released.

Ben reached toward a stump and knocked on it three times. He said, "Please."

They ate dinner in the living room, in front of the Franklin stove. The third time Ethan smacked his lips while chewing hamburger Stroganoff, Marge made good on her threat and marched Ethan into the kitchen, where he sat in the yellow light of one lamp and finished his meal alone. Ben and Marge, in the living room, said nothing; they ate and looked at the bright flare of fire visible where the stove doors met. Ethan's chair scraped, something creaked, and then there was a silence.

"Where's he going?" Ben whispered.

"Maybe his room."

"I didn't hear him on the steps."

"Well, there's noplace else to go. He has to go past us to get to the TV—"

"Yeah," Ben said, standing, "but he doesn't have to go past us to go *out.*"

"Ethan takes care," Marge said. "He wouldn't want to get soaked—oh, come *on*, Ben, he is *not* going to the river."

Ben said, "If the sump pump starts in now, to punctuate all this dread and criminality, I'll disconnect it." The sump pump started in, they heard it grinding downstairs. Ben said, "I can't disconnect it or the cellar will flood and the furnace'll go out."

"What dread?" Marge said. "What criminality?"

"No, it's just, with the river rising, with the goddamn *cellar* rising, I don't like it that we aren't together. Happy."

"Ben," she said, "do you know how unhappy he would be if there weren't consequences? Discipline? Rules he has to follow?"

"Yeah, but he can't follow them."

"He will. It's called learning."

Ben put another log into the stove and sat down again, then stood up. The sump pump was on. "But what if he does go to the river?"

"He won't. Go look for him if you're worried. It isn't such a big house, you know. Go look."

Ben sipped coffee and rubbed the back of his neck. "Do you understand that when you talk to me like that, when you patronize me, even if it's *Ethan*, I can't go do what I think is right?"

"You asked me and I told you."

"Bitch," Ben said. He put his coffee on the table in front of the sofa and went around it, clumsily and blushing. He leaned over, one knee on the cushion, to kiss her on the cheek chastely. "I forgive you your transgressions," he said.

Marge said, "Asshole." She held his head and stuck her tongue out slowly, and slowly licked his lips from side to side. Ben sat down beside her, moved in closer, and kissed her mouth.

"That's right," he said when they'd stopped.

"That's right," she said.

"Yes. As usual," he said.

"Yes."

As if to hold her trophy up, while Ben breathed deeply on the sofa beside her, Marge called, "Ethan!"

When there was no answer, Ben shook his head. She called again.

Ben shouted, as if in rage, "*Ethan!*"

The high small voice came back from far away: "Yes?"

"Where is he?" Ben said.

"Yes?"

Ben said, "Is that from outside? He *is* outside."

But Marge was already up, walking toward the kitchen and the cellar door, and she was on the steps before Ben had stood to follow her. Downstairs, in the light of the one bulb at the far end of the cellar, in the grinding chatter of the pump, Ethan swept water from the drain that Ben had uselessly capped. The water rolled with a loud hush across the gray floor and spilled over into the sump and was pumped out to seep back in again. There was a new smell downstairs, among the smells of wet wood and soaked stone and hot motor—the sharp tang of mildew. Ethan, in Marge's high black boots, continued to sweep. Marge in her fur-lined slippers, Ben in his still soaked boots, both with wet feet, stood watching him—the long pale intelligent face, the slender arms and legs, big hands. In Marge's boots, in the weak cellar light, in the pool of black water, Ethan looked very small.

"Hi," he said. Then he smiled, and his ill-brushed teeth shone beige.

Ben cleared his throat. "We thought you went out, honey."

Marge reached back to slap Ben's buttocks, to warn him into silence.

"How's it going?" she said.

Ethan said, "I don't think I'm making any progress. But you guys were so upset about the water, I thought maybe I could, you know, do something."

"No," Ben said, "you're doing fine."

"Really fine," Marge said. "You're a helper, all right."

Ben rubbed the back of his neck and stepped away so that Marge couldn't reach him. "Ethan," he said, "you know where babies come from?"

Ethan said, "Mom told me. You could check with her if you want to."

The boy swept more water into the sump, and the pump went on again.

"Okay," Ben said, "I will."

Marge turned and walked to the foot of the steps. Ben

stood, watching Ethan sweep. Then he turned too and followed his wife. When Marge was in the kitchen, and Ben was halfway there, Ethan called, "Hey, Dad? Dad?"

"Yes, sir."

"Tell me what she says, okay?"

That night the skies shook and darkness was total: no moon, no stars, no road lights visible from the bedroom window, the bedroom itself extinguished, and their eyes squeezed shut. They did not touch; when they rolled on the mattress or tugged at blankets or pushed a pillow flat, they grunted as if hurt. They slept finally, then awakened to hear field mice running in the eaves and between the walls at the head of the bed. It was the dry scraping sound of panic. It rhymed with the grinding chirr of the pump in the lath and beams and floorboard between them and the flooded cellar. Marge turned her bedside lamp on, and the walls jumped in toward them. Ben whispered, "Don't read. Just lie there. If you say you're awake, you won't be able to sleep at all."

Wearing Ben's undershirt and squinting from the blackened eyes of an exhausted athlete, Marge reached up to turn off the light.

"You look nice," he whispered.

"You always like me to wear your clothes."

"So I can own you."

"So you can *protect* me."

"Probably that too."

Marge said, "If the mice desert it, and come in here, does that mean the world is sinking?"

Ben said into his pillow, "The world will be fine."

After a minute, after another minute, with the dark-

ness humid around them and expanding into the darkness
of the flooded world outside, Marge said, "Can you
promise me that? Can you *promise?*"

"I promise," Ben said.

"You better mean that."

"I do. But no babies. No more babies."

She prayed at him: "Then you better mean it, Ben."

He wanted it to end with his praying back *I do,* but
he lay still and saw the yellow school bus, Ethan on
board, rolling off the rain-slicked road. Ben opened his
eyes so as not to see the children bouncing in the bus,
pips in a fat collapsing gourd. He saw the darkness.
He closed his eyes and against his will he looked closer,
supplying details, squeezing his eyes. He saw the
battered heads of bleeding children, and black hair,
yellow hair, brown hair, hair cut short and hair tied in
thin bright ribbon, all of it pasty with blood and teeming
with lice, the lice jumping in blood and tracking it tinily
on the wrinkled brown lunch bags that lay on cracked
seats and in muddy aisles. He heard Ethan cry, not in the
house with them now, but in his dream, in the future, in
the world that possessed more of him than Ben thought it
right to have to yield, and he pushed himself from the
pillow. He almost said *I do.* But he turned—Marge said,
"Ben?"—and in the darkness, with the pump going on
and off, with mice hurtling furiously between the walls,
he wrestled her, tore at the shared shirt, buried his mouth
in her neck and labored with his lips and teeth, dropping
upon her with no question and no answer, hearing nothing
for the first time that night, making what you might as
well call love.

A   NOTE   ON   THE   TYPE

The text of this book was set on the Linotype in Janson, a recutting
made directly from type cast from matrices long thought to have been
made by the Dutchman Anton Janson, who was a practicing type
founder in Leipzig during the years 1668–87. However, it has been
conclusively demonstrated that these types are actually the work of
Nicholas Kis (1650–1702), a Hungarian, who most probably learned his
trade from the Dutch type founder Dirk Voskens. The type is an
excellent example of the influential and sturdy Dutch types that
prevailed in England up to the time William Caslon developed his
own incomparable designs from them.

Composed by The Fuller Organization, Lancaster, Pennsylvania
Printed and bound by The Haddon Craftsmen, Scranton, Pennsylvania

Designed by Margaret M. Wagner